CW00688837

THE BATH SHORT STORY AWARD ANTHOLOGY 2017

THE BATH SHORT STORY AWARD ANTHOLOGY 2017

Compiled by
Jude Higgins, Jane Riekemann
and Anna Schlesinger

Published under licence by Brown Dog Books and The Self-Publishing Partnership, 7 Green Park Station, Bath BA1 1JB

www.selfpublishingpartnership.co.uk

ISBN printed book: 978-1-78545-226-0
ISBN e-book: 978-1-78545-227-7

Cover design by Elinor Nash
Internal design by Andrew Easton

Printed and bound by CPI Group (UK) Ltd, Croydon CR0 4YY

CONTENTS

INTRODUCTION

The Bath Short Story Award is entering its sixth year and almost 5,700 stories have been submitted since we began in 2012. There's so much creativity buzzing around the world and by the time this, our fifth anthology, is in print, we'll have published 90 of the most startling, original and wonderful stories — such a joy and privilege.

We are truly an international competition. In 2017 we received entries from 45 countries: UK, USA, Australia, Ireland, Canada, India, New Zealand, France, Germany, South Africa, Russian Federation, Switzerland, Spain, Hong Kong, Netherlands, Aruba, Belgium, Brazil, Finland, Italy, Japan, Malta, Singapore, Sweden, Angola, Armenia, Austria, China, Croatia, Cyprus, Denmark, Egypt, Indonesia, Israel, Lithuania, Luxembourg, Malaysia, Norway, Philippines, Portugal, Romania, Slovenia, Trinidad and Tobago, Turkey and United Arab Emirates. All the continents are represented, with the exception of Antarctica — perhaps the inspiration for fiction freezes at -50°C?

This has been quite a year. The political turmoil and unrest fanning out across the globe has provided a rich lode for writing and, although there were few stories explicitly on, for example, Brexit or Trump, the underlying themes have emerged in a number of the 1100 stories we received. Racism, discrimination, loss of identity and the displacement of people through war and poverty continue to resonate with writers, the best stories engaging the reader through powerful prose and possibly an unusual perspective. The same is true of stories about death, illness, dementia and growing old where finding a fresh angle can lift the subject.

Ultimately, the truth of the story is in the telling of it and writers explored a range of genres to do just that. Dystopia, magical realism, historical/science fiction and even the Western emerged from under a general umbrella of literary fiction. Although the majority of stories were in either the first or third person, a number of writers moved to the second person, which is notoriously difficult to handle but when done well can create a real connection with the reader. It was exciting to see experimentation with style, layout and contemporary forms of communication incorporated into the narrative. One story was entirely in text speak.

With such a range of styles, genres and subjects, it was not easy to whittle the entries down to a longlist of 48, selected by us and our reading team. From the longlist, emerged the shortlist and we were delighted that literary agent Euan Thorneycroft from AM Heath agreed to choose the winners and his comments on the three winning and two commended stories can be read in the authors' profiles. The winner of the Acorn Award was chosen by us; as many of the writers who enter are already successful in their careers, this award was established a few years ago to give unpublished writers another chance at a prize.

We hope you enjoy these stories. If they stimulate you to write, the 2018 Bath Short Story Award opens in November with details on our website bathshortstoryaward.org

We also work closely with Bath Flash Fiction Award and you might also check out their website for further inspiration bathflashfictionaward.com

Jude Higgins, Jane Riekemann and Anna Schlesinger
Follow us on Twitter @BathStoryAward
Subscribe on the site to receive news and updates on the competition.

ACKNOWLEDGEMENTS

The Bath Short Story Award is a team effort, supported by our keen and committed readers. Each story was read by two people from the team who recommended their favourites for the longlist. For the 2017 award we thank:

Anne Corlett
Paddy Edwards
Fiona Longsdon
Katharina Riekemann
Hannah Riekemann
Pat Robson
Diane Simmons
Dylan Spicer
Simon Toseland
Alison Woodhouse

Yet again, we are grateful to Mr B's Emporium of Reading Delights, Bath mrbsemporium.com for donating the Local Prize. In the current climate, where the arts have been given a backseat, Bath is still a literary beacon and lucky to have independent bookshops. Mr B's has won awards for its eclectic range of books and attentive service and is the traditional venue for our anthology launches in the autumn.

Local writer and artist Elinor Nash elenash.com won the 2014 BSSA and has continued to provide our artwork ever since. Each of the four anthology covers is an adaptation of her original stunning collage in a different colour. We thank her for her patience in providing an endless palette of colours for us to choose from and for her continuing support.

2017 JUDGE
EUAN THORNEYCROFT

We were honoured that Euan Thorneycroft, one of the senior agents at literary agency AM Heath, accepted our offer to judge this year's shortlist. He represents a wide range of fiction, from the highly literary to the more commercial and his constant goal is finding new exciting authors; prominent short story writers and teachers Cynan Jones, Vanessa Gebbie and Stevie Davies are among his clients. In addition to his agency work, Euan has been a committee member of the Association of Authors' Agents as well as the external examiner on one of the country's leading creative writing courses. He also judges the Bridport First Novel Award.

On receiving our short list, Euan commented, '*What a challenge? But an exciting one. The standard of the shortlist was very high and I would like to congratulate all the authors who made that list. Short stories are strange beasts – one day, a particular story might get under your skin. But on rereading, leave you a little cold. A detail that you passed over on a first read might make itself apparent to you on a second. I could only choose five winners but, rest assured, they all left a mark. I was looking for three things – originality, authenticity and confidence – and in the best stories here, all three of these were in ample evidence.'*

FIRST PRIZE
KATHY STEVENS

This Is all Mostly True

Mum says lying is wrong; Dad says white lies are okay; Stacie says fiction is lies and fiction is the best thing in the world but your mum's got a point.

Mum says to be polite and not have seconds unless I'm genuinely hungry.

Dad says to have fun, always plan ahead and wear the sort of shoes that I could run in if I needed to suddenly. Dad and I watch zombie films whenever Mum's out with the girls (it's our thing). The girls are all older than Mum; they have a lot of fun but rarely plan ahead, and in the shoes they wear they'll be the first to get their brains scooped out come the zombie apocalypse.

Mum's out tonight with the girls – she's just left. She said she's going to the bingo and will be back before ten. This means she'll be going out clubbing and will be back after one. Mum's rubbish at planning ahead and she tells lies of all colours.

She drinks too bloody much, is what Dad says.

I drink because your father's a cheating bastard, is what Mum says.

They don't say these things to each other. They say it to themselves and to me if I happen to be there at the time.

I like to watch Mum getting dressed in the morning. I sit on her uncomfortable, white-silk kidney seat and watch as she stretches and wiggles into her tights. I don't like to watch her get dressed when she's been out with the girls the night before because she often puts her foot right through her tights and they rip and she swears and shouts and her jagged big toenail sticks right through the nylon and I get upset and have an episode.

I've only kept with him because of you, Mum says, because I love you very much.

Mum feels obliged, because of me, to keep trying to love Dad. I'm an obligation. Stacie taught me that word and what it means. Stacie didn't say that I am an obligation, because Stacie's very careful with the truth. I like Stacie. She's thirty-three and quite poor, and she's got short blonde hair with pink ends and wears the most sensible shoes I've ever seen.

Dad calls Stacie 'lass'.

Dad's forty-four.

Thirty-three and forty-four are good numbers.

Mum's fifty-three which means she can't have any more babies. She had me fourteen years ago. I'm her first and last. Sometimes Mum sings My first, my last, my everything, to me and hugs me a lot. Sometimes she tells me to stop being weird and go away, especially when I'm watching her get dressed. She says stop it when we're in the supermarket or a park or in town and I start having an episode.

Dad says okay then, over and over. Okay then, okay then, okay then... like that.

I don't tend to have episodes when Stacie's over, so I can't remember what she says.

It's raining. I should go downstairs because there's washing on the line and Mum said not to forget to take it in if it rains. Dad always forgets. I forget too, but Mum tells us both so hopefully one of us will remember. She says for fuck's sake when we both forget to take the washing in.

Remembering to get the washing in when it rains is a 'basic thing'; I need to try to remember to be better at 'basic things'.

At least you've an excuse, is what Mum says to me when she's calmed down.

You've no excuse at all, she tells Dad.

I look out of my window.

The window's got flecks of drizzly grey rain on it, making the garden beyond it look greyer than it really is. The flowers in their beds are mostly dead or dying, but there's a crop of yellow roses which shine through the general greyness.

This is a good way of describing the window and the rain and the garden.

Stacie says I'm getting red hot at describing things and if she doesn't watch it I'll get a novel published before she does. This is a type of lie, but it's the nice type that friends tell each other. Me and Stacie are friends; we only tell nice lies.

Through the window, I can see the washing is still on the line.

I go downstairs.

I call to Dad and he says What?

Dad's having a fag out of the open front door. This is technically breaking a house rule, because he's smoking and his feet are on the carpet. Even though the wind is whipping the smoke away as soon as it leaves his nose and mouth, it's still breaking a house rule because his feet are on the carpet and that's what counts. Dad smokes and Mum drinks. I don't do anything. I wonder what it'd be like if Dad drank and Mum smoked. I think it'd be quieter.

I tell Dad the washing's on the line.

He says Okay, well.

I say I'll get it in.

He says Thanks Chuckyegg. This is one of his names for me.

I get the basket from beside the machine in the utility and unlock the back door and go out into the thrashing, wet cold. Stacie would like this description. If I remember I'll write it in my ideas book and tell her it later, so she can steal it for one of her stories if she wants to. Mum says stealing is wrong, like lying or smoking with your feet on the carpet, but Mum doesn't understand about fiction. Stacie steals my ideas all the time but she asks me first and I always say OK. She sometimes steals the whole of me, to be a character in one of her stories. I don't mind being stolen by Stacie. Stolen by Stacie, that's alliteration. Alliteration is effective when used sparingly.

I begin taking the clothes off the line. This is a plot point. I could just say I took the clothes off the line, but Stacie says that by using 'begin' before an action or activity, it suggests that something will happen while the action or activity is being done by the protagonist.

A protagonist can be anyone interesting who you'd like to follow around.

Nobody ever follows me around, apart from the neighbour's dog, Heinrich. And that's only because I throw treats over the hedge for him and look after him when the neighbours are away.

Heinrich is a German name. The neighbours aren't German. Heinrich's name is ironic. I don't know how Heinrich would feel if he knew he had an ironic name.

I'm half-way through removing the washing from the line when a very good-looking boy comes into the garden through the side gate and right up to me and says You're ever so pretty, would you like to be my date for my friend's party. I drop a sock.

This is called action.

It hasn't really happened, so it's a kind of lie, but it could have done, which means it's credible. Credible lies are just fine in fiction.

If the boy was ugly, the author – that's me – would have to work harder at giving him a three-dimensional personality so that the reader can invest in him.

He could be someone I know or a stranger.

He could even be a zombie.

If I wanted to introduce some emotional complexity, he could be the zombie of someone I know. That way, I'd be scared for my life but also sad about killing him.

Maybe Dad would hear a commotion from where he's having a fag at the front of the house and run around the back to save me.

The zombie could kill Dad or... for even more emotional complexity, it could bite Dad and then Dad could kill it but later I'd have to kill Dad. That would be a major plot point and emotionally complex. If I didn't notice Dad's bite but the reader did, that'd be called dramatic irony. Dramatic irony is different to regular irony.

But then, if Dad was still having a cigarette out of the front door at the time the zombie came into the back garden via the side gate, Dad would've seen it and a whole lot of action would have been avoided.

Fiction is complicated. But Stacie says it's easier than real life.

I've finished taking the washing down. I haven't folded anything because it's not yet dry. I'm using my initiative.

As I go inside, I linger for a moment at the back door. One foot on the concrete step, one on the lino inside. The rain has stopped already; I needn't have bothered getting the washing in at all. I hear Heinrich's bark from behind the neighbour's hedge. Everything smells of petrichor.

This is excellent writing.

The scene takes place in the fictive present (me on the step) while also alluding to an alternative future in which I hadn't brought in the washing, and Mum never noticed. The bit about Heinrich barking is good because we've heard about him earlier, and the bark suggests the passage of time.

Also, it's a moment of introspection.

Readers love introspection because it's like listening to a friend, and a lot of readers are lonely.

The use of petrichor is a gamble, because most people won't know what it means. But one difficult word shouldn't put off most readers.

Writing stories is like The Emperor's New Clothes, Stacie told me before I wrote anything at all. She said Nobody wants to admit their ignorance. I wish everyone explained things like Stacie does, I'd never be confused again.

Stacie left three hours ago, before Mum. It still smells of Stacie in the hall. Her perfume is called patchouli. Mum says drug addicts wear patchouli to hide the smell of marijuana. Mum says mean things sometimes but she can't help it because she's sad. Nobody told me this so it could be wrong. It might be wrong but it's not a lie.

What's the movie, I ask Dad who's finished smoking and is in the kitchen making malted milk.

Malted milk is our favourite drink. And it's alliteration.

Lady's choice, says Dad.

Dawn of the Dead, I say.

Not again, says Dad.

Evil Dead, I say.

Hmm, says Dad.

Evil Dead 2, I say.

Sold to the little lady in the camouflage onesie, says Dad.

I'm the little lady in the camouflage onesie, so I go into the living room and find the film, pop it into the DVD player and read the back as I wait for Dad and the malted milk.

I've seen Dawn of the Dead twelve times and Evil Dead seven times. I've only seen Evil Dead 2 three times, so I don't know it verbatim yet. Verbatim is a great word; it's Latin and most people know what it means.

My favourite movie is Shawn of the Dead, but Dad won't

watch it with me anymore because we've seen it nineteen times and he's sick to the back teeth. Mum thinks it's strange that all our favourite movies have 'dead' in the title.

Is there extra sugar in it, I ask when Dad comes in and hands me my mug.

Nooo, he says in a silly voice and winks. This means there is.

People lie all the time and it's not always bad. Lies can be funny, like Dad lying about the sugar. Lies are only really bad when the stakes are high.

You can kill a vampire with a stake, but not a zombie. You have to cut a zombie's head off, or shoot them through the brain with a large calibre bullet, or blow them up.

I'm about to press play on the remote control, but change my mind.

What is it? says Dad.

Don't know, I say.

This is a lie.

Go on, I want to see this flick. I'm dying to know what happens, says Dad.

This is a joke.

I told Stacie she's my best friend today, I say.

Oh, says Dad.

Yes, I say.

Dad puts his malted milk on the coffee table between us. The mug says: BEST DAD IN THE WORLD.

This is a lie.

That was a nice thing to say, he says.

Yes, I say.

What did she say? he says.

She said, you too, I say.

That's great, he says.

It's a lie, I say.

Elsie, your leg, he says.

I know, I say.

Have you taken your meds, he says.

Yes, I say.

This is a lie.

She's only my friend because I can't go to school and you and Mum pay her to come here, I say.

My foot is banging against the leg of the coffee table and it's hurting but it won't stop however much I tell it to.

Dad moves his malted milk from the table to the floor. A safe distance. He tries to prise mine from my hands but my fingers have gone stiff and won't move an inch. This is a cliché. Clichés are a sign of bad writing.

Okay then, says Dad. Okay then, okay then, okay then…

Kathy Stevens was born near Stratford-upon-Avon in 1991. She has a BA English Literature from Bath Spa University, and is the recipient of the Kowitz Scholarship at UEA, where she's near to completing her MA in Creative Writing. Her short stories have appeared in *Litro, Prole,* the *Bath Short Story Award 2016* and *Bath Flash Fiction Award* anthologies, *Supernatural Tales Magazine, The Literateur, The Cadaverine, Patrician Press* and *Firefly*. Besides writing, Kathy is a keen guitarist and music fanatic, who enjoys 1950's fashion, rock'n'roll dancing and anything involving boats. She's working on a literary novel about a dysfunctional family.

Euan Thorneycroft commented:

'I loved this story from the word go. Both funny and heart-breaking. We are immediately grabbed by the unique voice of Elsie, a teenager with unspecified personal problems (although this point is never laboured), and who reveals her acerbic family dynamics through frank observations.

It leaves its emotional mark by offsetting the casual, frank tone of the narrator with the obvious severity of her episodes, the frictions of her family home and the sad sense of her isolation. Elsie's absorption with storytelling is, on the surface, an inventive, amusing lens, but it becomes a desperately sad force for the reader as her difficulties show through behind that drive for escapism. It finishes with a gut-

punch as her fascination with writing has equipped her with a language to articulate the distance between her and the rest of the world. A writer of huge confidence.'

SECOND PRIZE
MARY GRIESE

Performance in the Hills

Black widow on her golden horse, that's what they call me, riding the boundaries of my hill farm. It takes an hour; my horse has fast Spanish blood. He turns to gold when he loses his winter coat and as for my coat, I always wear black. Nothing to do with Owen's death a month ago, I love black. I'm keeping going, little choice.

First I change the sign on the old gate at the end of the track. I've just bought a small power drill which also works in reverse and to my delight the rusty screws fly out of the *Ewes in lamb – please keep dogs on leads* board. The sign is peppered with shot from the feral boys who only make for the footpath if they see me. The fields are crisscrossed with footpaths from the days when men came down off the mountain for work.

I'm fixing *All loose dogs will be shot* to the gate when I see a string of boys attached to the electric fence, an elf-sized boy bouncing in the middle, hurting, laughing, screaming. He's scrawny, impossible to age, anything from eight to twelve, hair too wild to conceal sticky-out ears, little face the colour and texture of a prune, no effort to visualise him as an old man. I retired well before he was born, but as a teacher my heart went out to children like him, scallywags we called them then. I probably taught his father.

They're way off the footpath. I'm too weary to be cross and they're not harming anything but themselves. I'm just feeling satisfied with my new drill and the straightness of the sign on the gate. Whenever I caught myself on the fence, Owen would say a little electric shock sets one up for the day. These boys are hanging on for dear life.

Gathering up the pieces of the old sign, I remember how we'd agonised over the wording. Dear Owen determined to be respectful, thinking they'd respect us in return. They didn't. The last dog killed two ewes and mutilated four. The police begged Owen not to bring any more dogs to the police station and, though subtle with their wording, more or less told him to shoot any future killers. 'If the owners cared they wouldn't let them out'.

I'm not about to shoot a loose dog. I'm merely making a stand.

I was going to make a stand over the pups, it wasn't necessary in the end. I was fuming with Owen, he'd forgotten Meg was on heat and left her in with the dog. We have four working sheepdogs, quite enough, and the thought of finding good homes for puppies gave me nightmares. The litter of six was born a month before he died. I was beside myself, only two suitable people had shown a vague interest. Some might say I was overreacting.

Owen understood and made a difficult move to save my sanity: the evening they were born he came in from the barn and quietly announced there were just three pups; he couldn't leave Meg with less. He went straight up to the bathroom and I heard him vomit three times. We never spoke of it.

Now eight weeks old, two have gone. Usually bitches are the first to go, but the last pup has a lot of white on her body and a strange face divided down the middle, half white, half black with orangey brown eyebrows. She's a barrel, Meg did them well.

I have her in my arms when a van long overdue for the scrap-heap rattles into the yard and five grim boys in their late teens get out. The track is long and rough, I can imagine their tempers should a boulder hijack their tyres. The elf boy is here and a taller wizened boy who has to be his brother. They're looking for a pup and heard I have some for sale.

I go cold, immediately picture half-starved dogs on chains, shut in old cars, their horrible van. A bitch to breed from will prove lucrative. The format of our meeting is like a stand-off: I tuck the pup deeper inside my black cardigan and step back, the bolshie buyers edge up for a bargain and we move round as if spoiling for a fight and I don't think of saying she's sold or spoken for. Since Owen, I'm in a fog.

Playing for time, I ask, 'Do you keep sheep?' I mean their fathers. There are colliers in the village with commoners' rights to run a few ewes on the mountain.

'Yes,' says the little one.

'Many?'

I think he says sixty and his brother may say a hundred and fifty but as they speak as one, I don't quite catch the numbers. So they're liars.

'It was my husband's dying wish I keep this one,' I say, red-faced, fingers crossed. 'Her ancestry is good on both sides. Don't know how I forgot, his death is so recent I'm still in a fuddle. Sorry.' Forgive me, Owen.

The boys shuffle their feet and glare at me and my lie. I can now expect gates wrenched off hinges and sheep out. They return to the van in silence, slamming doors with killer strength. The engine starts. I turn my back on the dust storm and name the pup Fly.

The last vehicle to leave the yard with such drama was the ambulance.

I'm creeping up on elf boy. He's the only one I can see, the others are still making their way through the trees, shouting their orders and I have enough Welsh to understand what they're saying. He's standing at a field gate holding a stick, one of the few gates with metal posts. I've lost enough weight to be hidden by a scrubby tree.

When they came for the pup he was the only one to venture close, as if keen to stroke her and I had inklings he may have loved her. Not that he was going to get the chance.

I'm hesitating. I so badly want him to refuse his hideous instructions. I wonder why the boys are yelling when I could be around, and how they know there's a nest in the post. I didn't and I'm the nature lover. It was my subject.

He slides his left hand towards the hole in the post and I'm on him. Both hands gripping his coat collar to bash his tiny brains out. Head on metal. 'Evil little bastard,' I hiss an inch from his face. His head hits the post. Just once. I'm shaking. No one appears. No one jumps to his rescue. My hands squeeze his throat, fingers overlapping. He's spluttering, choking, 'I wasn't going ...'

Then I see I might kill him and stop.

He slumps to the ground in a heap, limbs in all directions and starts to cry. Shuddering violently, I sit on the ground and lean against the post, terrified and heartbroken we could be so brutal. Him and I. But then he didn't carry out his orders, I'm the only savage here. God almighty I'm afraid of myself. The boys' shrill voices ring in my head: 'Throw the birds into the air high as you can, we'll hit them with the sticks as they fall. One at a time, mind.'

I'm sobbing now. Minutes pass. I picture Owen's disbelief and sadness. Verging on hysteria, I'm unaware of the boy crawling towards me. A gentle tap on my arm, I drag my sleeve across my eyes. He's sitting next to me. 'I wasn't going to do it,' he says quietly. 'I was going to say they'd flown, that the nest was empty. That's why I had to get here before them.' He takes a dirty packet of cigarettes from his pocket, shakes one half out with the panache of a practised smoker and offers me. I shake my head.

All boys smoke here, one at my school boasted having his first fag at three. He lights up knowing I'm in no position to disapprove, his skinny hands trembling. We stand up together our bawling over and hear the loud tweeting coming from the post: babies desperate for food. I can't speak. I move away, he follows and a blue tit begins her frantic descent through leafy branches.

I think he's telling the truth. In that pitiful screwed up face, I see two clear amber eyes beseeching me to believe him and I'm thinking for heaven's sake and he rubs the back of his head and his hand comes back bloody. I go to whisk him round and he jumps back. Quite rightly, I'm a mad woman.

'It's okay,' he says. 'Head cuts always bleed more, I've had worse.'

I sink back against a tree. 'I saw red,' I say.

'What?'

'It's a saying, when you're incensed a red mist covers your eyes, blinds your actions.'

'Not to do with blood then?'

'Probably. I must look at your head, please.'

He turns obediently. His hair needs no parting and the small cut I inflicted has almost finished bleeding. That's because he's young. I cover my face in shame. 'I'm sorry. I'll make this up to you. Somehow.' We sit for a while in silence, apart from the faint rustle of boys lurking in the undergrowth. One thing, I won't give him Fly.

'Can I ride your golden horse?' he says, wide-eyed at the thought.

I don't ask if he can ride, here all boys ride. Some fathers own shepherding ponies, there's still one private mine with pit ponies coming up for holidays and certain ponies on the mountain can be caught by the wilier boys.

I nod. He's off, aiming for home through the fence they've bent down, realises and doubles back to use the gate. I need to shout after him, say he can only ride if I accompany him, explain my horse is sensitive, lively, strong. But I can't shout, his little figure is so tiny.

I usually walk last thing at night. Not far till I tuck Fly under the arm of my black coat,

Meg always jumps up; she'd like to be there too. The only white on us showing is the tip of Fly's cheek and the blaze down Meg's face. I'm not nervous in the dark. The boys may be around, but if they did witness my behaviour that day, I'll be left well alone. Labelled crazy.

Meg stops dead and gives a little growl and I see minute lights twinkling in the field next to the farmhouse, the one sloping down to the river. The boys light fires there, stick potatoes in the embers, sit for hours by the water, drink cider and smoke. Other times they favour the woods, live in dens with thick walls and watertight roofs woven from bracken and hay, these boys are skilled. I never know where they are. Owen compared them to cats: swift as panthers and changing territory whenever the fancy takes them. Our cat, my cat, favours the sofa for a month then tiptoes through the photograph frames and takes up residence on the windowsill for the next month.

The moon is half full. There's movement at the bottom of the field. I shush Meg, place my hand on her head and we stand perfectly still at the gate. A low blue haze is wafting across the fluff of a thousand dandelion clocks and phosphorescent shapes are emerging from the riverbank trees.

Owen's choice of return was as a barn owl, mine is a pampered cat. We were always talking about reincarnation, though neither of us believed, it was a form of comfort. But I've already seen him once at twilight with his huge white wings.

This is no owl. There are two beams of light a yard apart, separating and coming together, travelling slowly and eerily up the field. I hold my breath and don't move. My horse materialises through the mist. An apparition walking between the pearly lights lifting his legs ridiculously high as if stepping out from underwater and I wonder if he's crossed the river. Chiffony clouds seem to rise with his glistening hooves, spread into streamers and disperse. The little dot of a figure on top has no saddle or bridle, his legs stretch across the horse's back, but don't reach halfway down his sides. He's holding a small torch in each hand, quietly waving them out to the side then back, one at a time, to the left, to the right and my beautiful horse is responding. Moving gracefully to the direction of the lights, obeying this little creature on his back and I'm shaking more than when I attacked him. They sway and twist in elegant circles. Elf boy is skilled.

My golden horse in a night circus. Then a swoop of glorious white wings, so few flaps necessary for such a glide along the trees. The ringmaster.

They don't see me, I'm in black.

Mary Griese is a novelist, short story writer and artist with an MA in Creative Writing from Bath Spa University. She is currently seeking publication for her debut novel *Man in Sheep's Clothing* and is represented by literary agent, Jane Conway Gordon. Her memoir, *Sand on the Mountain*, won third prize in the Fish Memoir Prize, 2017. She has written articles for The Guardian and farming magazines. Thirty years ago, while running a sheep farm on the Black Mountain, she formed her arty business: 'Slightly Sheepish'. She recently published and illustrated a picture book: *An Alphabet of Farm Animals*.

Euan Thorneycroft commented:

'I thought this story was one of the most individual of all that I read. A recently bereaved woman, alone on her farm, dealing with her grief. There's a heavy, heady atmosphere to this piece, the tone being set from the captivating first line, with an almost dreamlike quality in places. But the author doesn't overstep here. The story is also grounded in the reality of rural Wales. The depiction of this rural landscape feels totally authentic. I loved the seemingly small, but keen-eyed observations that appear along the way – a blue tit's frantic descent through the branches, the young boy changing direction to take the gate rather than the bent down fence. I think the emotional tone is handled incredibly well. We don't dare feel hopeful at the close, but the vision of the young boy working with the horse –

in the dark – and the widow unseen and ignored is a beautiful and haunting ending. I found this to be a story that got better and better with each read.'

Third Prize
SARAH MACKEY

Forget Me Not

'Crocosmia,' says Virginia.

It is softly exclaimed but Henry, one ear cocked, is yanked from sleep and halfway out of bed before he realises that he is awake. For a moment he sits there, clutching his juddering ribcage, one leg on the floor, his ragged gasps filling the moonlit room.

Virginia is standing by the window, a pale, silvery phantom, staring down at the garden. She has the stillness of sleep around her but she is not sleepwalking. She rarely gets more than a couple of hours a night now.

'It's Crocosmia Henry. Crocosmia "Lucifer",' she says. 'Next to the Hostas and that white flowering Hebe.' And he remembers. Remembers her bewilderment the previous afternoon when she couldn't name the fiery little blooms. And the sudden anguish, the heartbreaking, unreasoned anguish, as the word had continued to elude her. Anna had tried to intervene but he had bustled her back in through the french windows.

'Go home darling,' he'd said. 'I'll sort her out. It'll be fine.'

Anna had twisted in his arms to watch her mother rocking backwards and forwards on the lawn amidst the scattered teacups. A peaceful afternoon shattered.

'But she's always forgetting words. What's wrong with her now?'

Henry had resented that 'now'…

'Not her garden, darling. You know that. The garden's different.'

And so it is. No matter how forgetful Virginia has become in the two years since her enforced retirement, no matter how many friends' faces she has misplaced or memories that have slipped down the back of the sofa, how many times Henry has found books in the fridge or mugs in the washing machine, the garden has always been a bright refuge in her increasingly foggy world. Often, when events threaten to overwhelm, they sit on her favourite bench by the bee garden and gradually, magically, Virginia's body loosens and her panic subsides as she names each shrub, each perennial, each wildflower, with the same fond confidence she used to have pointing out her ex-pupils in the marketplace.

Until yesterday.

'Come back to bed,' he says. The adrenaline is still pumping through his body but his mind is drugged with fatigue and he can't make himself get up to join her. Slowly he collapses backwards onto the pillows, his caftan rucked up and one foot still out of bed. He can sense, rather than see, Virginia drifting across the room towards him. She smells of earth and lavender. As she gets under the covers she is whispering softly:

'Crocosmia, Osteospermum, Tradescantia, Valerian, Buddleia, Spirea… Myosotis. Myosotis. Myosotis…' It is a charm, he thinks; a defence against the invading hordes that creep up to steal her away.

Henry sleeps late the next morning. It feels as if just moments have passed but the moonlight has gone and bright sunshine is pouring into the room. He is alone and the house rings with silence. He no longer trusts himself to wake whenever Virginia wanders, so last month he had new locks fitted on the front door and windows, and the wrought iron gate from the garden down to the river is padlocked. The keys are dropped into the dusty copper umbrella stand each night and fished out with Henry's ornately-carved walking stick before breakfast. He won't hide the key to the back door though, whatever Anna says. What if there was a fire or he became ill? The garden will look after her; she will always be safe there.

Virginia is lying spreadeagled on the lawn in her nightdress, her face turned towards the sun, smiling as she soaks up its energy. Henry waves from the bedroom window, but she's not looking at him. Around her the garden shimmies in a light breeze, its beds, banks and planters full of summer colour, the air already humming with insects. Paved pathways lead off the lawn to sheltered spots under the fruit trees, and tall shrubs, steps and stone walls break up the space. As Henry watches, a blackbird bounces on to the grass, head tilted, tail up. It takes no notice of Virginia, hopping fearlessly between her feet as if she were just another piece of stonework.

It has always been Virginia's garden; Henry hasn't a clue about planting and pruning. In the early years she was the one who gave it shape, carved out its borders and boundaries, mothered it with tenderness and discipline. As it has matured, she has gradually stepped back, giving it the space to flourish in its own way.

'She loves that garden more than me,' a teenage Anna had complained, so many years ago. Henry, looking down from his window, suspects that nothing has changed.

Two days later it happens again. They are wrapped up against an unseasonal breeze, drinking coffee outside the french windows, when Henry suddenly becomes aware that Virginia's soothing monologue has meandered to a halt. Squinting into the sun, she rises and crosses the lawn to the banked bed running diagonally from the east wall to the steps. There she runs her hand gently up green sword-like leaves and taps her fingers against deep orange-red flowers. She breaks one off and rubs it into her palm.

'What is it?' Henry asks, but Virginia avoids his eye.

'Oh Henry… you are a hopeless old thing. I told you… I told you its name the other night. All these years and you still don't know the plants.'

But Henry can't remember. It takes him twenty minutes to find it in the RHS encyclopaedia, while the coffee cools and Virginia treads nervy loops around the lawn.

'Crocosmia.' She rolls it around her tongue as if trying out a new flavour. There is no light of recognition in her eyes. 'Crocosmia.'

Later Henry locates his multi-coloured Post-it notes and writes the plant name out in capitals. He sticks one on the fridge, one to the frame of the french windows and one to the plastic box of gardening gloves that sits by the back door. He contemplates putting one on the bread bin — Virginia has taken to storing her trowels and secateurs in there — but the words 'Bread Bin' are inscribed in black swirls on its cream ceramic surface and he doesn't want to cause confusion. Anna, in helpful mode, has already placed pre-printed stickers on most of the kitchen appliances. Several now have stuttering scrape marks down them and Virginia's pruning knife has an undiscussed stickiness on its serrated blade.

At the weekend Anna drops in, laden with cakes and good advice, and immediately spots the Post-its. Virginia is outside, staring again at the vivid red flowers, surrounded by tones of terracottas and yellows.

'Kniphofia,' she says, 'Helenium, Achillea millefolium, Potentilla…' And then she pauses, brow furrowed.

'Myosotis?...'

'I'll make a map,' Anna says when Henry explains, 'or we can put little name sticks in — those lovely wooden ones from Godden's. Don't worry Pa. Leave it to me.'

Henry wants to say 'no' but it is too late. Anna is determined to save the day. She hums and smiles her way through the afternoon, seemingly impervious to Virginia's occasional tart asides and non sequiturs. Henry has seen it before — that bright cheery air that comes when a project, a chance to do good, takes away the need to talk to her mother.

'You really don't have to, darling.' A last ditch effort as they are clearing up together. 'I know how busy you are.'

But Anna's hug silences him, her solid optimism brooks no dissent.

He senses trouble as soon as they return from their day out the following Tuesday. A familiar little sea-blue Golf sits on the driveway. Anna has let herself in and has spent the morning at the patio table, calligraphing flat wooden marker pegs. Each peg has a plain central stem for writing and green, leaf-like, protrusions on each side. They litter the main bed like Armistice crosses. On a large sheet of paper Anna has sketched out the shape of the bed and the individual clumps of each perennial. Across the top she has written the words 'Forget Me Not' in three dimensional letters and she is now busy colouring a border of small blue flowers. Henry looks at his middle-aged daughter and sees pigtails and freckles.

'I ran out of markers,' says Anna. 'I didn't realise how many we'd need. I'll get some more at the weekend.'

Virginia leans into the foliage, in what has recently become her usual spot. She pulls up the tag next to the Crocosmia and frowns at it. Then she grabs the next, and the next...

'Mum, don't do that.' Anna is using her gentle voice. Henry winces.

'Don't...' he says, but he's not sure to whom. The word

hangs in the air, unheeded.

'Anna, dear,' says Virginia crisply, ruthlessly lucid. 'This is not a council park. We are not... tourists.'

Each little marker comes up with a shower of earth and a sharp inhalation. Anna sits statue-still, head down, hand still grasping her blue felt-tip pen. When Virginia dumps the pegs on top of the unfinished map, soil sprays onto Anna's arms and dress. Still no movement. Henry watches helplessly, heart stretched between the two women as Virginia stomps inside. Both are crying. Neither sees.

'Well, this will come in really handy,' he says brightly, sweeping the pegs off Anna's drawing. 'I'll put it up on the fridge and...' But the tears and the earth have already mingled in swirling smears and his gentle rubbing just makes it worse.

When Anna has finally gone Henry finds his wife crying into a soil-stained tea towel in their bedroom. He wraps his arms around her brittle, bony body and they rock back and forth in silence. Virginia eventually nods off and Henry goes outside to find a spade.

At first the plant seems to fight back, it has spread much further than he realised and there are corms everywhere. The evening air is cooling the sweat on his neck by the time he makes his last trip to the compost heap. All done. Problem solved. Time for dinner.

The next morning Henry wakes with an absurd feeling of lightness, of joy. His limbs feel supple and surprisingly pain-free as he stretches them over to the empty side of the bed. From the window when he rises he can see Virginia sitting on the lawn, watching the blackbird as it rummages about in the big patch of fresh-turned soil, next the Hostas and the white flowering Hebe. She is clutching something but he can't see what.

Henry goes downstairs and brews the coffee. As he moves in a waltz-step around the kitchen he scrunches up the Post-it notes and gives himself a little cheer as they land on target in the recycling box. He can hear Virginia's soft chanting from the garden.

'Spirea, Helenium, Kniphofia, Potentilla... Hebe... Myosotis, Myosotis, Myosotis...' Then a silence.

A shadow falls on the chequered tile floor.

'Henry,' says Virginia, appearing in the doorway, 'the Crocosmia... it's gone.'

She takes his arm and pulls him gently outside. He feels a sharp twinge of pain in his back as they slowly cross the lawn, and then another, unrelated to digging, somewhere near his sternum. As he stares at the small wooden marker peg, bright against the rich dark soil, Henry mourns the years to come, a succession of little deaths and uprooted memories, as the garden gradually disappears. He clings tightly to Virginia's hand.

'Myosotis,' prays Henry. 'Myosotis, Myosotis, Myosotis...'

Sarah Mackey grew up in the West Midlands and lives in London. Over the past year she has attended creative writing courses at City Lit, which has inspired her to write short fiction. Sarah was longlisted for the 2016 Words and Women prose competition and has been selected for inclusion in the *Between the Lines Anthology, 2017*. Forget Me Not is her first published story.

Euan Thorneycroft commented:

'A beautiful, sad study of a family buckling under the weight of memory loss. Virginia's memory has been fading out for two years, forcing her into retirement and pulling away many of her relationships. Her beloved garden is the last sanctum of peace and stability, and through Virginia's husband Henry, we feel the pain of its loss, and the conflict as their well-meaning daughter repeatedly gets the tone wrong in her attempts to help. The husband's love for his wife and his desolation at the end of the story — after a brief moment of hope — are extremely moving. As is the strained relationship between mother and daughter. This is a well-constructed story.'

LOCAL PRIZE & COMMENDED
CHLOE TURNER

Breaking the Glass-blower's Heart

The door closes behind the family, softly, as if the fingers of the person on the other side have lingered on the handle. Then Camila is alone, on her knees among the shards of the shattered vase. A bare patch in the dust up on the mantel's leaden-grey marble hints at the vessel's usual position: given pride of place, with its sloping shoulders and its pinched waist. A heart, a glass-blower's heart. Now, some small splinter of glass hunkers under Camila's right shin, threatening to break the skin, as she leans forward to pluck the fragments, one by one, from the reluctant fibres of the rug.

The largest piece is as big as the palm of Camila's hand. It curls up there like a sharp-edged bowl. Blown glass with a swirling bolt of blue; it reminds her of a fresco in the Basilica back home, the many-towered cathedral which dominates the far bank of the Ebro from her mother's tiny flat. Something of the blooming skirts of Goya's Queen of Martyrs, captured here in vitreous, bubbled transparency. She thinks back to times when she gazed up at the dome's fresco as a child: sliding along the cathedral's smooth pews with her head tipped back, while her father ran soft cloths over gilt angels, and mopped marble floors around the sandalled feet of the day's last tourists. And then, when what was left of her small clan gathered under the dome for the first Dia de los Muertos after her father's death, she remembers wondering who would dust the angels now.

There was no question in Joanne's mind as to who smashed the vase, and why. She called Camila – screamed for her – from the front room. Camila had to leave the children alone at the kitchen table. Not that they were concerned: they barely looked up, busily fashioning a rocket from the badly-rinsed contents of the recycling bin.

Tiptoeing amongst the fragments in stockinged feet, Joanne was already at fever pitch by the time Camila came through the door. It was a fight about much more than the vase, of course, but that alone could have done it. Camila has no idea how she provoked it, but distrust has festered between them from the start. Since the day Camila arrived, Joanne has winced if the girl so much as looks at her work, her shoulders hunching as if judgment has fallen before Camila has had a chance to say a word.

Ironically, Joanne's artistry is the one thing she admires about the older woman, most of all the blown glasswork which emerges like crystalline mysteries from the iron-roofed workshop at the end of the lawn. Left alone, Camila has often run her fingertips over ripple-edged vases and bowls, and over those strange, interconnecting forms – purple, bleeding into green, bleeding into blue – brittle sea creatures worn smooth and stranded on the piano's lid.

Joanne was just drawing breath – the eye of the storm – when the two women heard a squeal; the screech of the table's feet across the slate tiles, and the muffled thuds of two sets of footsteps up the few stairs from the kitchen.

'She broke it...'

'It was mine. He took it...'

'I had it first...'

'No...'

Camila's arm shot out without thinking, a barrier across the entrance, preventing the children from straying onto the broken glass. Owen began to squirm at once, never content to be contained. Beca's shoulders were shuddering with tears. Camila bent to squeeze them still, and the little girl nuzzled into her neck. Joanne was frozen, mutely pained, the field of glass between her and hers.

'David.' Joanne broke her silence to yell for her husband. Her eyes didn't leave Camila's. Upstairs, there was the squeak of boards from one side of the ceiling to the other, as David made his way to the landing and down.

It didn't start like this. Should never have turned out like this. The day Camila arrived, the whole family piled up to Stansted to meet the plane. Owen's orange jump-jet t-shirt was the first thing Camila saw when she walked into the Arrivals hall, dazed after a bumpy landing and the glass of cheap Tempranillo the businessman beside her had insisted she join him in, before rubbing his fat fingers up her thigh.

The children loved Camila from the moment they met her. They mobbed her, giggling at the brightly foiled frutas de Aragón she unwrapped for them, tiny paws pulling at the short lace skirt she was already regretting, as the reality of a British summer's day took hold. David was solicitous: kissing her on both cheeks, snatching up her bag, refusing to take the trolley further. Joanne rolled her eyes, asked about the journey, patted Camila on the arm – stiff, but not yet unfriendly. Camila thought of her mother's enveloping arms, and reminded herself that six months would pass quickly.

It was not just that skirt, of course – it became apparent quickly that few of her clothes were suitable. Joanne urged her to go shopping, at her expense; to buy more. (To cover up.) There is no shortage of money here. Whatever David does in that glass-fronted box in the city, it pays for this comfortable Victorian villa. For the fridge with its doors which open like an embrace. For the sleek car on the pavement outside, which is treated to waxes and steam-cleans as if it were some pampered pet. And for her, Camila, of course; David has paid her well. She has sent home 400 each month, leaving tear stains on the letters her mother has sent in reply. But despite Joanne's fluttered notes and hints, Camila has found herself hardening to the weather. Donning tough soled boots under floating dresses as a sole concession to autumn's approach. Even folding that lace skirt over at the waist so that the lower half of her thighs, still deep copper from a summer spent waitressing in a Tarragona beach café, are bare to the breeze.

She and David were thrown together from the start. He likes to be home to bathe the children each night, and Camila, unsure whether it was her place to do so, got into the habit of kneeling by his side. Only rarely did Joanne displace her. Joanne's working hours are erratic, so that the children would sometimes go days without seeing their mother, and Camila found herself offering cuddles and kisses in compensation. Joanne blamed the tyranny of the glass. When using moulds, she preferred to cast at night, she said, free from distractions. And the concentration required for free-form sculpting left her exhausted and vague, wandering through the kitchen in her heavy overalls, calipers or a length of blowpipe still clasped in one grey kevlar mitt.

Joanne would often miss dinner, leaving Camila and David to eat alone, and then perch later on a stool with a sandwich, answering David's enthusiastic questions – technical queries, about melting points, crimping and annealing, desperate attempts to break the ice – in short, staccato bursts. She is thin, Joanne, painfully so, and on the rare occasions she leaves her long, pale neck unwrapped in scarves, her clavicles protrude like the wing bones of a bird. Camila has never seen them touch each other. Sometimes David reaches a hand towards his wife, but she always skids away under it, as a silk cloth slips over glass.

From time to time in these past months, Joanne has gone away. For a weekend usually. Some weeks ago, she stayed away for five days. There was no warning, though David spoke of a conference as if it had been long planned. In Joanne's absence, Camila grew bolder, stretching and then breaking the strict rules by which Joanne imposed herself on the household. Camila let the children dress themselves, mixing colours and patterns as they chose, swapping Beca's bland t-shirts and skirts for bright dresses with ruffles and bows, which she found in the midweek market in town. She allowed the children to stay up late, and when David returned from work, delayed by the train, he found them dancing in the formal front room, bouncing on the sofas' plump cushions, their faces flushed and high. He ushered them out, gesturing towards the glassware, but he laughed as he chased them up the stairs.

On those evenings, Camila began to cook food from home: spiced longaniza sausages, with fried eggs and migas, and almojábanas, pastries flavoured with sugar and anise. When David opened a bottle of wine with dinner, she accepted a second glass. On the night before Joanne's return, he opened a second bottle.

Camila pulls a final fragment of glass from the matting now. It is cold down here on the floor, as if a void beneath the carpet is sucking the heat from the room. She folds her arms under her small breasts and sits back on her heels. Tiny slivers still glitter amongst the rug's fibres, but they will have to wait for the Hoover's indifferent grasp.

She didn't know – why should she? – that this vase was Joanne's favourite. That it was the first vessel David's wife blew unaided. That the wrap of blue that curled through the heart was drawn from a cobalt cane Joanne chose for her mother's eyes. But he knew. And it was not Camila who left the door to the front room unlocked, the heart-shaped vase lifted down from its place on the mantelpiece to a side table, where it stood no chance against Beca's exploring fingers and Owen's aeroplane arms. She saw his face when he came in – reluctant, but he was prepared to take the blame. David had stoked this fire.

But Camila didn't let him. Instead, she nodded at Joanne's accusations, let the outburst envelop her, impressed by the heat that had risen up in this brittle woman. David, beside her, visibly diminished as his wife spoke; he was weak and insubstantial now. Camila watched him shift his weight from one foot to the other, his fingers fidgeting along the undulations of the radiator behind his back.

And when Joanne finished at last, shoulders slumping with the effort of the invective but still defiant, Camila knelt at her employer's feet. She plucked the first of the fragments, lining them up on a folded newspaper beside her knees, while the family shuffled out around her. Beca slipped free to reach for her, but it was David who pulled the little girl back, shepherding her into the hall. Through the closed door now, there are fragments of a conversation: Camila hears 'flight', and 'morning'. 'That girl', and 'mistake'. A taxi being booked for an early hour.

Camila picks up the largest shard again, with its drape of spun cobalt inside. She wraps it in a tissue, the blue even more vivid against the white. Sharp edges subdued, she tucks it into the pocket of her skirt. By sunset tomorrow, Camila will be back on the banks of the Ebro, back in the arms of her mother. But she will take with her something from the glass-blower's heart.

Chloe Turner's stories have been published in online and print journals including *The Mechanics' Institute Review, The Nottingham Review, For Book's Sake Weekend Read, Kindred, Halo, The Woven Tale Press,* and *Hark.* 'Long-gone Mary' was published by InShort Publishing (Australia) as a standalone chapbook in 2015, and *Waiting for the Runners* is one of a series of six chapbooks available this autumn from TSS Publishing. Chloe won the short story category of the Fresher Prize 2017, was shortlisted in the Exeter Short Story Prize 2017, and received a Special Commendation in the Elbow Room Prize 2016. She tweets at @turnerpen2paper, and blogs about books and writing at www.turnerpen2paper.com

Euan Thorneycroft commented:

'This is a very confident story of a young Spanish au-pair finding herself working for a middle-class family in England. The breaking of a vase ripples out so that we see the strained dynamics of this tense little pocketed family, with its suggestion of infidelity and lovelessness. This is a very well-written story, full of fantastic descriptive detail.'

THE ACORN AWARD FOR AN UNPUBLISHED WRITER OF FICTION

SANDRA MARSLUND

Everything Must Go

The nights are the worst. She is restless in the cavernous bed that she doesn't yet fill. Sleep is brief, consumed with the lumber of dreams and broken-edged sections of the past that stir and heave in the undertow. Tonight she sits up in the blackness, but doesn't know why. Maybe her leg strayed to the cold side. Maybe it was the tapping in the attic again. She thinks it began yesterday, but she can't be sure. Did she dream it? She looks nervously at the ceiling, waiting, holding her breath. But there it is again. A gentle tat, tat, tat in the corner above the wardrobe, like small hands knocking. There's no magic in this world, she thinks. Everything has an explanation. Wind perhaps? But the night is clear and still. She sinks back into her pillows and breathes in the smell of sleep and old hair. This is when she would have leaned over and prodded him, gently of course. *I think there's something in the attic.* He would have grumbled. Told her it was all in her head. But he would have gone up to check all the same. She is not ready for such valour. Hasn't been up there since the day of the fall. Instead she pulls the pillow over her head, and tries to count her breaths. She can still hear a noise, only now it sounds more like soft scratching, distant and muffled. Later, in the greying light, she wakes to silence. She is almost certain she was dreaming.

Winter

As she chops onions alone in the kitchen on Christmas Eve, she remembers things. How his arms wrapped around her from behind, how his soft lips brushed against her neck and the barely audible *I love you* in her ear. She sips her wine and realises she's already three-quarters of the way through the bottle. *Was it really so bad?* She eats in silence while Ruby spears sausages and stares at her phone. She tells her to put it down. Anything to resume some sort of family tradition around the dinner table. It's too late of course. The damage has been done. Ruby just rolls her eyes and looks back at her screen. Later the two of them walk side by side through the cold air, down to the moss-clad church in the village. They scuffle past tightly packed pews looking for empty spaces. She feels eyes flicker over her and look away. She thinks people are whispering, but she can't be sure. Husbands and wives and children huddle in neat files, one after the other after the other. They take their place right at the back, next to the drunks and the old man with no teeth. Ruby refuses to sit down and hangs back, shoving her hands in her pockets and fixing her eyes on the floor. As a few strained notes swell from the organ, there is a general shuffle to rise. The men stare ahead, the women, look around, catching one another's eyes and smiling. But they don't look at her. And she feels like a gypsy caravan parked in a row of shiny houses.

As they file out back into the night, Sue and George from next door appear behind them. Sue grabs her arm and pulls her aside.

'So sorry to hear about the accident,' Sue hisses in her ear. 'Awful bad luck that. Didn't I say so George?' George nods and stares at his shoes.

'And to such a lovely man too.' Her breath smells of boiled egg.

'Now don't you go up on that roof. George will finish off that tiling for you, won't you George? Just say the word.' She can feel their eyes on the back of her head as she and Ruby make their way back up the lane. She picks up the pace until she can see the glow of the hallway light in the distance.

Tonight the tapping is louder than usual, a slow, dull thud, echoing into the dark hours. Rain? Hardly. The stars were out and rain doesn't fall on starry nights. Perhaps then the rain of past days collected in some blocked gutter, now dripping through the roof on the pots of old paint on the attic floor? A trick of domestic acoustics? *Just one of your stupid dreams.* She sneaks into Ruby's room and climbs into her bed, pulling the duvet tight across both of them like she used to when Ruby had nightmares. She closes her eyes, willing herself to calm down. To stop the trembling. At some point Ruby squeezes her hand.

Spring

Water begins to mutter in the pipes. The boiler chokes and grumbles cholerically in the utility room. One day it falls silent. The dishwasher spews water over the cracked tiles and the kitchen drawer comes away in her hand, cutlery clattering to the floor like gunfire. Outside, the garden is a tangle of knee-high grass and bindweed. In the far corner, the fence nods in the wind, revealing glimpses of Sue and George's begonias. *It takes two to keep a family you know,* her mother's voice resonates in her head. The house is in agreement. *Told you so,* it bellows from every room. And still the tapping. Too real and clear for ghosts. A trapped bird? She lies too afraid to move, too afraid to hear. She will just let it stay. For as long as *it* is up there, and she is down here, what does it matter? Two can live side by side without ever touching, without ever meeting. She will buy ear plugs.

In the greenhouse she makes a start on clearing the tangle of overgrown tomato plants. Along the shelves, dried wisps of some larger vegetable sprout and droop over terracotta pots. Perhaps she could plant something new? Below, on neat rows of metal hooks, hang all his tools, each one labelled in the familiar black font. *A place for everything and everything in its place.* She winces at the wooden-handled trowel. Remembers an argument. His meaty hands tugging at her jeans and pushing her face against the glass. In the receding sunlight, she spots the sucky imprint of her hand on the window pane. She tries to wipe it off, but it sticks like tentacles.

Summer

Something catches her eye at Highbury's Furniture Stores in the high street. *'Summer sale – everything must go!'* emblazoned in red across the shop window, a thick line under the *must*. She peers in at the jumble of furniture in the display. Lamps, wicker chairs and sea-themed prints, all stacked around a giant white bed. It is the sort he would have hated. An old-fashioned brass type with twisted railings and copper bed knobs, dressed in layer upon layer of flouncy cotton and frills and piled high with cushions the colour of frosting. Like a giant wedding cake. She thinks it knows nothing of fear and bumps in the night.

Inside she asks the shop manager for the price.

'Of course we always recommend that both you and your husband try it out first. You know...to check for *firmness*.'

'No need,' she says. 'It's just me.' She speaks the words slowly, rolls them round in her mouth and balances them on her tongue, like she's trying them on for size. He leers at her from his frameless glasses and takes her credit card.

She is hopeful when it arrives late one afternoon in August. She watches the deliverymen dismantle the old bed and carry it away, swaying and sweating from its bulk. She is hungry for sleep. Once they have left, she adds new sheets and fat pillows, building layers of throws and cushions like she's seen in a magazine. She stands back for a second to admire her work, then hurls herself at its centre. Lies spread-eagled trying to reach the edges with both hands. Stares at the ceiling and drinks in the silence.

But in the night the tapping returns, bolder and jolting, knock, knock, knock. Realer than real. Ghosts? What nonsense. A fallen lamp, grating and rattling in the wind. She sits up in the moonlight, arms folded. Attempts a mental recollection of the contents of the attic: boxes of Ruby's baby clothes, the suitcases, wallpaper rolls and tins of paint, a crate of old cables that no longer plug in anywhere, but which was kept, just in case. Standard attic matter. Nothing to worry about.

She is brave in the early morning light. She opens the hatch and hauls down the ladder with one hand. She asks Ruby to hold it steady. Ruby hesitates. *Like you did when dad went up on the roof?* Ruby's eyes hold hers, and she wants to drown herself in their pools of grey, right there and then. They stand rooted, eyes locked, neither of them moving, neither of them breathing. She is the first to break away and starts to climb the rickety frame. Too late for recriminations. What's done is done.

The attic is a musty, airless tube. A shaft of sunlight pierces the narrow crack in the roof. The one he was going to mend. She looks around her. Just as she thought; piles of junk, once useful, now mere detritus of a past life. Cardboard boxes, stooped and grey with filth, a bent golf club, his mother's pine chest of drawers, a plastic Santa Claus. And there, underneath the cracked light, a pair of scuffed, brown brogues and a bag of white shirts. She breathes in the familiar scent of Burberry and sweat. Above them, hanging on the wall and twisting in the breeze, is his squash racket. Her stomach heaves. He must have put it there the last time she threatened to leave. She yanks it off its hook and fingers it in the dim light. Can still feel the whip of it across her face. The chequered imprint on her cheek. The taste of blood and tears on her tongue.

For it must surely be that, swinging against the wall whenever the wind is up? She tries it out for sound, banging it against the side. A solid knock of wood against plaster. It's almost the same. And yet, perhaps not quite the hollow clang that has been stealing her nights. Bile surges in her throat and she shivers in the thick heat. Her hands work quickly as she gathers his clothes and drags them down the ladder, piece by piece, shoving them into bin liners held taut by Ruby's hands. Perhaps it's time to convert the attic. Make a new bedroom. Rent it out. Everything must go.

Later, she takes a hatchet to the chest of drawers and makes a bonfire in the garden. They watch in silence as the flames flicker and swell with each armful of stale fabric. A plume of smoke, thick as tar, billows into the peach sunset. They save the squash racket till last. It spits and crackles like lard.

Sandra Marslund is a translator of Danish and Norwegian books and commercial texts and also contributes book reviews and literary articles to national and local publications such as *The Guardian, Mslexia* and *Manor Magazine*. She has always written, but only started writing 'seriously' after completing an MA in Creative Writing from Exeter University in 2016, for which she received a Distinction. She recently began entering her short stories to competitions, where she has been both long and shortlisted. This is her first award, and it has spurred her on to complete her novel. She lives in Devon with her two teenage daughters.

The BSSA team commented:

'Great suspense and structure in this story, which builds, as the seasons unfold over one year, to an unexpected revelation. The striking last line says it all.'

COMMENDED
FIONA RINTOUL

North ridge

Gone four o'clock. So, it's true then. Or is it?

From the car you can see the path I took this morning.

That's where I'll come from. When I come.

The path is slick with milky ice. The overhanging pine branches sparkle with snow. Maybe not a great day for the hills. Not a brilliant time to tackle the north ridge. But I'm an experienced winter walker. I have crampons, an ice axe, all the gear. And it was beautiful earlier, pale winter sunlight glinting on snow. Sometimes, those are the best days. If you're happed up. And you've got the gear.

The sun is slipping beneath the horizon now, tingeing the clouds tangerine and rose – daubs of colour in a monochrome winter's night. It's going to snow again. You can tell.

Where am I?

'Mummy,' says Euan, 'will Daddy be back soon?'

'How should I know?' you snap. Then you twist round in

the driver's seat and smile at him in the backseat, regretting your sharp tone. You thought he was asleep. If only he would sleep. He looks very separate, sitting there in the back of the car, snug in his green down jacket and purple woolly hat, clutching Hamish, his worn old teddy bear that used to belong to me. 'I don't know exactly when he'll be back, sweetheart. Soon, I hope.'

Scream. You could scream. Or cry. That would be normal in this situation. But you don't. As you knew you wouldn't. As I knew you wouldn't. My wife, the stoic.

Or do I even think like that? Who knows? I've become a stranger.

To you.

To Euan.

To myself.

That's what happens.

If you did scream, no one would hear you. The camp site is deserted. It's November, for Christ's sake. The camp site owner laughed when you phoned to book. You can camp there if you like, but I'll not be there.

The shower block is locked, one toilet left open for the likes of you.

And me.

The likes of us.

You washed there this morning, standing on a towel and balancing on one leg as you struggled to get first one foot then the other into the tiny metal wash hand basin, flinching as freezing water coursed over your already mottled skin. You didn't even bother to make Euan have a proper wash. Just wiped his face with a flannel.

As the colours fade from the clouds, it starts to sleet. Dollops of water slap against the windscreen. Each one holds its shape for a second then dribbles down the glass.

You pick up your phone and check the screen. Two bars of signal. That's enough. But there have been no messages. No calls. Well, maybe I don't have a signal up there on the north ridge. But I should be down by now. That's the thing. I should have been down long ago, skidding along the icy path towards you.

And our son.

Your son.

In some languages, the pronoun 'you' is different in the singular and plural. French, for example. *Vous* is plural; *tu* is singular. Your son can be translated as *votre fils* or *ton fils*. In English, the pronoun stays the same. That's something to be grateful for, isn't it?

'Mummy, can I sit in the front?' Euan asks.

'In a minute, sweetheart. When this goes off.'

Euan sighs. 'I'm fed up,' he says, more to Hamish the bear than to you.

You lean over the driver's seat and rearrange one of his soft brown curls. He's such a good boy. So patient. Everyone says so. You're so lucky.

We're so lucky.

'Do you want a drink?' you ask.

He shakes his head.

'Why don't you draw a picture? You're such a good wee drawer.'

'Alright.' He sounds like he's only doing it to please you.

You rummage in the glove compartment for his paper and crayons. You should have had another child while you still could. Why didn't you? All the alleged obstacles – work, space, money – seem meaningless now.

But it's okay. It's fine. You have Euan.

And Euan has you. A pronoun that need not change.

The sleet is turning to rain and getting heavier. The remaining light is a chilly grey. You stare at the blur of hills through the misting windscreen, starting to hate them.

It's amazing how quickly rain melts snow. Water is now dripping from the pine branches, creating pools on the icy path

I took this morning. The path will be treacherous if it freezes over.

And that's the way I'll come.

When I come.

The light is fading fast now. Only the melting snow staves off total darkness. Should you phone or leave it? The number is written on a piece of paper stored in the glove compartment. I gave it to you before I set off this morning.

'In case of emergencies,' I said, gazing into your sea blue eyes.

I've never done that before. Given you a number to phone. I didn't say why this time was different. And you didn't ask.

Why didn't you ask? Because you knew.

Slabs of silence. Grimaces of pain. Tell-tale.

'Don't ring too soon,' I said. 'If I'm not back.'

Now is too soon. You know that.

You turn the key in the ignition, put on the windscreen wipers and turn on the headlights. In the beam of the headlights, you see our lone tent bending and flapping in the gathering wind. Perhaps you should take it down. All our things are inside. Our Thermarests and sleeping bags. Our food and spare clothes. Our books and reading glasses. Our camping stove and plastic mugs are tucked inside the vestibule door, waiting for someone to unzip the tent, crawl inside and brew a panful of tea.

It was cosy in there last night. We held hands across our sleeping bags. I asked if you were warm enough. You said you were toasty warm, and I said: 'These goose-down sleeping bags don't owe us anything, do they?'

'Mm,' you said, and we fell asleep listening to the wind buffeting the nylon flysheet with Euan curled up between us on his own small sleeping mat.

It would be good to take the tent down before the snow melts, and it gets even darker. But you can't take it down now. Not in this weather. You'd get soaked bringing the things back to the car. And what about Euan? He'd have to wait in the car on his own. Better do it later. When I'm back.

You turn off the windscreen wipers and the headlights. God, it's dark without those twin beams of light.

Where am I?

'Mummy,' says Euan, shifting in the back seat, his drawing abandoned on the seat beside him, 'I wish Daddy would hurry up.'

You turn and tell him what you must tell him. 'He'll be here soon.'

Then you say, 'Give me those crayons if you're not using them. They'll make a mess of the upholstery.'

'I'm fed up,' he says, but to you this time, not Hamish.

'Why don't you lie down then? Have a wee snooze. You must be tired. That was a very long walk we did.'

'Not as long as the one Daddy's been doing.'

'No, not as long as that.'

'Daddy's been doing a proper hill,' Euan disclaims proudly.

'So he has.'

'The north ridge.'

You grin at him. 'That's right.'

Perhaps you're remembering how happy I looked this morning as I shouldered my rucksack, adjusted my walking poles and folded my map into my waterproof map case. A man on a mission. A man setting out to do the north ridge. It must be written somewhere in the Book of Time that fathers of small children shall one day do a proper hill again while the children's mothers take them on easier walks, for you know of no example of it working the other way round. Not that you minded. Not this time. Not today. The walk up to the lochan with Euan was beautiful. You saw red deer loping through glittering snow, a stag and five hinds, a harem in the making.

At least that's what I hope.

Afterwards, you walked along the pebble beach in front of the fishing village and skliffed stones in the sea.

You did do that, didn't you?

And over fish and chips in the village hotel, you told Euan about the white-harled fishermen's cottages behind the beach.

'They're called the twelve apostles, and each one has a different shaped window upstairs. Do you know why? So that the fishermen could tell if there was a light on in their house when they were sailing home after a hard day's fishing.'

Perhaps Euan asked what the fishermen did if there wasn't a light on.

Perhaps you said, 'There was always a light on. The fishermen's wives put a candle in the window to welcome them home. They were looking forward to seeing them.'

And Euan said, 'I'm looking forward to seeing Daddy.'

And you ruffled his chestnut curls and said, 'So am I.'

The rain has stopped now, and the moon has appeared. But it's just a sliver. It hardly gives any light. You can barely distinguish the black hills from the indigo sky.

'Mummy,' says Euan, 'Daddy said he'd be back at three and it's nearly five.'

'How do you know it's nearly five?'

'It says so on the clock.'

And so it does. The luminous green digits on the car clock, which I changed to the twelve-hour clock so Euan could read it, say five to five.

You must have left the ignition on when you turned off the windscreen wipers and headlights. What if the battery's flat? You depress the clutch and start the engine. It turns hoarsely a couple of times then sputters to life. You touch your head to the steering wheel in relief.

'Can I sit in the front?' Euan asks. 'You said I could sit in the front when the rain went off, and it's gone off now.'

You smile at him in the rear-view mirror. Such a good wee boy. It's his teatime now. He must be hungry. And tired. But he hasn't complained once.

Our son.

Your son.

Ton fils.

'In a minute,' you say. 'Why don't you lie down for a bit?'

'I'm not sleepy,' he says, stifling a yawn.

Of course, I might be lost. I might be in trouble. I might have fallen. The north ridge is tricky, especially in this weather.

What then? What if there has in fact been an accident?

Perhaps you remember the look in my eyes when I set off this morning. The way I said goodbye. The way I embraced you and stroked the back of your head. The long moment when I picked up Euan and held him close. The way I closed my eyes and buried my face in his curls, inhaling his scent.

There have been spaces. Private spaces. Things not discussed.

But you know me. You know my limits. You know what I can and cannot take.

I cannot take the rot inside me. I cannot take pity.

I cannot let my son watch me waste away.

You glance behind you. Euan has fallen asleep, stretched out on his back, one arm flung back above his head, the other wrapped round Hamish. You lean your arm round the seat and touch one of his soft brown curls. Then you put on your woolly hat, pull on your gloves and take the number I gave you from the glove compartment. Softly, you open the car door and get out, clicking the door shut behind you.

Outside, the air smells of wet earth and encroaching night. You zip up your down jacket against the wind and pull your hat down over your ears. You take your phone from your jacket pocket and check the screen. Still no missed calls. No messages. You slip the phone into your pocket and gaze at the darkness where the path is that I took this morning.

That's where I'll come from.

When I come.

If I come.

You walk away from the car. The dark is suffocating now.

Night has fallen; you are falling too.

It's time to phone. You must phone.

The nearest town is only a couple of miles away, but you feel entirely alone. Wildlife rustle and squawk in the undergrowth. You can no longer make out our tent. Only the thrum of the car engine charging the battery provides a measure of solace.

Inside the car is our son.

And he is clutching a worn old teddy bear called Hamish that used to belong

to me.

Once you phone it will be over. That's the thing. You will become you singular. Euan will become your son. Ton fils.

But it's dark now. It's time to phone. You must phone.

You take your phone from your pocket. By the light of its torch, you read the number I gave you. You pull off your right glove and punch in the number.

Fiona Rintoul is a writer, journalist and translator. She is author of *The Leipzig Affair* and translator of *Outside Verdun* by Arnold Zweig. *The Leipzig Affair* was short-listed for the 2015 Saltire first book of the year award and serialised on BBC Radio 4's Book at Bedtime. Fiona's most recent book, *Whisky Island*, a non-fiction title about the Isle of Islay and its whiskies, was shortlisted in the 2017 Fortnum & Mason food and drink awards. Fiona lives in Glasgow and on the Isle of Harris.

Euan Thorneycroft commented:

'A short story with a brilliant, powerful conceit which packs a real emotional punch as we near the inevitable ending. We are sucked into the claustrophobic wait as a woman minds her child in a car, coming to terms with what she knew from the day's outset: that her husband did not intend to return from his mountain climb.

The decision to tell the story from the husband's point of view is a brave one. Are these the real-time thoughts of a man dying of exposure, his only comforts, the clammy car below, where he knows his wife waits, bracing herself against the agony of accepting her loss?'

HARRIET SPRINGBETT

Big Bones

My name is Marie and my seven sisters are called Marie too. It's because of Maman: she's French, you see. She probably hoped we'd be good all our lives if she named us after our Virgin Mary, though I'm not sure it's working very well for me. You might think it's complicated for us – all being called Marie – but in fact it isn't because we use our middle names. Luckily, they're different.

I'm eight, I was born in 1969 and I'm the youngest. I think I was a mistake because Maman had run out of middle names by the time she pushed me from her stomach. I'm just Marie: Marie-nothing Smith. I don't know what name she'll choose for a new baby.

If you're thinking that Smith isn't a French surname, you're right. That's Dad's fault because he's English. He had a dream so we left France last year and came to live on a farm in Dorset. Everyone in France said it rained all the time in England but our Virgin Mary laid on the hottest ever English summer so we wouldn't be homesick.

It sounds as if Dad is to blame for something else, too, and that's my bones. I know, because he has just told Maman so.

The milking bail is a good place for me to spy on them. Dad

bought it in a farm sale and towed it home behind the tractor. There's enough room to milk three cows, so it's a luxury for our Twinkle – and for Maman, because now Twinkle stands still. The only time Maman isn't rushing around or writing letters to our aunts is when she's milking. That's why Dad comes here to talk to her. It takes him a long time to say things, but that's okay because it takes Maman a long time to reply.

'She's got my bones,' Dad says.

I expect Maman to say, 'Don't be silly,' to Dad, like she does when I say stupid things. I wait for her to say, 'Don't be silly, she's got her own bones, not yours.' But she doesn't. She doesn't say anything at all, which is a bit scary. It either means she agrees with him, or she's thinking. All I can hear from my hiding place in the feed bin is milk squishing from Twinkle's teats into the tin bucket. I can't see Maman's face from in here, but there seems to be an agreement-silence going on between them. It doesn't sound as if it's a good thing to have his bones.

'And she says she wants to be a dancer,' Dad adds.

The squirting stops. It's difficult to tell what kind of silence it is now, but it definitely feels louder. I squint through a rusty hole. The bin is just big enough for me to sit inside when it's empty. It's easy to climb into because the lid on the top is broken. I can slide it open, check there are no rats inside and then slide it closed above me. The only problem is that I can't see much. I can't see Maman's reaction.

I'm sure Dad is wrong about my bones. If anyone has given me bones, it must be Maman because I'm the same height as her. Here in England everyone's taller than Maman. I think that's why she's cross all the time. The ladies in the village shop, where I sneak to read *Jackie*, say she's 'petite'. The way they spit out the French word they've stolen from us and drop the last 't' makes it sound like an insult.

Maman starts milking again, but she still hasn't said anything. I wish she'd given me her hair as well as her bones. I love Maman's hair, even though it's going grey. It's silky like the edge of the blanket I rub with my fingertips to get to sleep. Dad fell in love with her hair. Well, with her plaits. She lost them on the ferry when we moved to England. I looked everywhere for them, even overboard, but I couldn't find them. Dad made her go to the hairdresser as soon as we arrived, to tidy the straggly ends, and she looked all English when she came out. So now she doesn't have plaits, only her hair. Dad doesn't seem to be sad about it, though. He's been happy since we left France, unless he's just pretending because it was his dream and not Maman's.

Each time Maman mentions her lost plaits, they are longer and fatter. One day, when she was yanking tangles out of my ginger mop, I told her it was nice to think they carried on growing in her memory. She rapped me on the head with the back of the brush and told me off for talking too much.

I'm always being told off, unlike Noelle and Thérèse. They're my closest sisters, not that they're close to me in anything but age. I watch them all the time when I'm not watching the animals or the insects or the plants or the sky or other people. Maman said they were too young to stay in France with our big sisters and our six aunt Maries, even though they're four and five years older than me. They're never told off. They cover for each other. It's because they are UTTs. In case you don't know, that means Unidentified Telepathic Twins. You didn't know, did you? Our Britannica is the only encyclopaedia in the whole world with the definition in it. I'm certain of that because I added it myself.

No one else knows that Noe & Thé are UTTs. I worked it out as soon as I learnt the word 'telepathic'. I reckon Thé stayed inside Maman for a year after Noe was born. She waited until Noe told her that Maman had thought up another middle name before she came out too. And they're telepathic because they don't have to talk. They just stretch their eyes or jerk their heads. When I copy them they don't hear my silent words. They just look down their long noses at me and shut their bedroom door. I think Dad must have shared his nose bone with them.

At last, Maman replies. 'Her bones are big. Too big for a dancer.'

Too big? I imagine my bones sticking out of my skin. If

they stuck out I wouldn't be able to dance. I wouldn't be able to do clouds, though my trees would be much better than they are today. There's definitely nothing sticking out. Not yet. The bones in my elbows aren't far from the surface and I've always had a doubt about the knobbles in my ankles. I hope they're wing bones and that feathers will break through one day so I'll be able to fly like the Greek boy in our Britannica. I can't look at my ankle bones properly right now or I'll disturb the empty sacks and Maman will hear the rustling and tell me off for eavesdropping, and I'll say I wouldn't need to eavesdrop if she bought us a television.

Maman's milking squirts are faster now. My hands remember Twinkle's floppy, leathery teats. They feel dead, like when you hold your index finger against someone else's finger and stroke them both together.

I wonder if I can change my bones? Or find another body to live in, like a hermit crab? I like dancing the crab. I like the scuttle and rattle of them.

Twinkle stamps her foot. I picture her tail swing and swat Maman's cheek, and my bottom twitches. When Maman milks Twinkle, she presses her face into her flank and sometimes a Jersey hair sticks on her cheek and then falls into our soup. I think she's listening to hear when Twinkle's stomach has no milk left in it. Cows have got seven stomachs, you know. They make milk with one, calves with another, cowpats with the third and they chew cud from the fourth. I don't know what they do with the other three.

'Anyway, if she wants to be a dancer, she'll need lessons,' says Maman. 'And we can't afford them.'

I gather some loose dairy nuts into a pile with my fingertips. I don't want dance lessons. Katy Dean has dance lessons. I've seen her in her horrid pig-pink tutu and I wouldn't be seen dead dressed like that. The kind of dancing she did at the school show was boring little steps and jumps to cassette music. I couldn't see what she was dancing. It was just Katy Dean showing off.

In any case, I don't need lessons because I'm already a

dancer. Louis told me so. He said I was a real dancer and not the stupid copycat Noe & Thé say I am.

It's true that I do copy things. Not just some things: everything. I don't know if it's a gift, or a curse a witch gave me when I was born. I can't help myself. As soon as I start to watch something I feel myself slip into it, like cake mix when I tip it into the star mould and it runs into every corner and fills it. When I dance the beech tree I flow up the trunk and along the branches to the twigs. I stretch out my arms and watch my fingers turn into leaves. They unfurl like in the nature film Mr George showed us on the new colour television at school. And when my finger-leaves are open, the hollows in the centre of my palms begin to flower.

I don't know if you see what I mean. It's difficult to explain with words. Louis understands. When I dance, Louis can see exactly what I'm dancing. He even guessed right when I danced the octopus, which is hard because it has eight legs. I've always danced. I used to dance with Minou, our French cat, before I even knew I was a human. She and I would lie on the rug in front of the fire, twitching our ears when someone came in and swishing our tails when Noe & Thé bothered us. Maman used to tell us off for climbing onto the table and I had sores in the corners of my mouth from licking my whiskers.

Dad grunts. There's a clack-clack as he slits binder twine and I listen to him stuffing a slice of bale into Twinkle's haynet. He doesn't say any more about bones or dance lessons.

By the way, Louis is my best friend, the only person I share my orange Space Hopper with. He's my cousin and he belongs to my Aunt Marie-Jeanne, even though he didn't come out of her stomach. He was an orphan, like our lambs. Tatie Jeanne got a bargain when she bought him.

I wish he could live here. On the last day of his last visit I hid him in my secret hideout in the gap under the hot mouldy hay bales in the barn. I told Tatie Jeanne he was dead and that she'd have to go back to France alone. But Noe & Thé dragged him out and brought him back. Tatie Jeanne hugged them.

Maman smacked me. And Louis looked sad.

Maman slaps Twinkle's rump. She's finished milking.

'Poor Marie. She'll never be a dancer,' she says. 'She hasn't got the physique, thanks to your big bones.'

So it's true: I've got Dad's English bones. And I'll never be a dancer. I scrunch up the handful of nuts and crush them. One of my nails scratches the side of the metal bin but I don't care if Maman hears me.

Twinkle kicks the bucket, making a clang echo around the tin milking bail. It's so loud that I miss Maman's next words. Dad leaves. I hear him squelch through the mud outside.

Louis must have been wrong when he said I could dance. Maybe he only knew what I was dancing because he's telepathic with me. He might be an OWT – that's a One Way Telepath. And before you ask, I don't know if OWT is in our Britannica because I've only just thought of it.

Louis never said I'd need lessons. He never said I hadn't got a physique or that my bones were too big. Perhaps he doesn't know anything about dancing.

Dad squerches back into the milking bail. He doesn't say anything to Maman. There's a waiting-silence. I can't see them through the tiny hole. What are they doing?

The feed bin lid slides open a sliver and I cower into the corner. A long handle thrusts through the gap. Metal prongs stab. I scream.

Maman shrieks and flings off the lid.

Dad shouts a word I've never heard before and yanks up the pitchfork.

I explode from the feed bin like a volcano. Red lava dribbles from holes in my calves.

'Oh, Marie,' sighs Maman. There's pity in her eyes, and I know it's not because of the blood.

My molten heart cools into stone. I have to dance, even if my bones are no good. I want to dance. No matter what happens, I'm going to dance.

Harriet Springbett lives in rural France with her French partner and teenage daughters. Her debut novel, *Tree Magic* was published by Impress Books in March 2017 and she is now seeking representation for her second novel. Harriet grew up in West Dorset and qualified as a manufacturing engineer before fleeing to France in 1995 to escape machines and numbers. She studied French at Pau University but only became bilingual when she met her partner, who taught her slang and rude words.

DAVID BUTLER

Speak No Evil

'The trauma is here,' the neurologist says, 'you see?' Her biro is tracing a circle about a darkened area to one side of the monitor. A Rorschasch test, say. A walnut, infinite space bounded in a nutshell. I'm here at the mother's request. Jamal is my student.

'So what does it mean?'

'It's early to say. With trauma to the frontal lobe there may be some loss of movement. Down the right hand side.'

'Bloody racists!' says the father.

'Also,' she lays down the biro, nods slowly, 'there may be impairment to the speech function.'

'Bloody racists!' Mr Shafiq is a ferocious man with a pot-belly. It's his fourth time to say it. His wife, the dentist, has a deep thumbprint of insomnia beneath each eye. She asks, 'In what way, his speech function?'

'He may have difficulty with sentence structure. Forming sentences.' The doctor rubs her left temple, is explaining something or other about the Broca area. But I'm picturing the last time I spoke with Jamal; a good-looking lad, raven-haired, a flash of white teeth. Impossible to square that image with the damaged moth flickering on the screen. Though I too am well acquainted with the devastation of brain trauma. My cousin, Andrew. For twenty years Aunt Mary has fed him baby food with a plastic spoon; Uncle John silent, stern, reading it as divine judgement.

The word 'aphasia' pulls me back to the present. 'With this kind of aphasia, the patient is very often aware of their condition and can become intensely frustrated. *Everyone* will need to be patient.' She directs *'everyone'* toward Mr Shafiq.

Before we leave I look in on him again, lying as though asleep on the gurney, so vulnerable in the thin hospital gown. Once I've waved off the Shafiqs' taxi, I return to have a brief word with the Garda. Is there a chance of charging anyone over the attack?

'In this town? See no evil speak no evil is the motto of this town.' The best hope, she goes on, though shaking her head, is if, afterwards, the victim can give us some kind of a description. Afterwards.

I'm filled with anxiety flutters. They're something I've become increasingly prone to. Hard to believe the skull, that cage of infinity, can be so fragile. A single boot to the head had done the real damage. On a whim I walk out as far as the People's Park; allow my thoughts space to wander. *Trauma* from the Greek, a hurt or a wound. Though *Traum* in German means dream. I've heard it said the amputee dreams he is whole, that each waking is a new amputation. What dream will Jamal wake from? And wake into? Or my cousin Andrew, for that matter?

The police tape is gone from the bushes where the attack took place. On Friday evening, about half past eight. It wasn't even dark. Today is Sunday, and the low clouds and hint of rain have the place half empty. All the same, even with rain imminent, there are still people about. A man and dog over by the footbridge; a woman with a push-chair; a couple of teens bent like street-lights over their i-phones. Impossible to think no-one witnessed the attack.

See no evil, speak no evil.

Looking up, a line from one of Jamal's stories comes to me: *The sky was pregnant with rain, and before we got home the waters broke.* That's how he was: witty. A witty individual. Something of an all-rounder, too. He played cricket, and was a winger on the college soccer team.

What was it brought him out here, to this place?

A memory, something I'd seen and shouldn't have seen, grips me. Jamal and Danny Keane behind the bike-shed. My office overlooks it. I'd assumed they'd gone there for a sneaky fag – you weren't supposed to smoke if you were on the soccer team. What I saw wasn't a kiss, not quite. Not technically. But Danny's hand took the back of Jamal's neck with exquisite tenderness and drew their heads together. Together they rested, perhaps a minute, then with a pat to the cheek they broke. Would he know what had brought his team-mate out here? Padma Shafiq has her dental practice out the Dublin Road, that much I know already. Where Danny Keane lives I can find out handy enough – the dad runs a call-out plumbing business.

The address turns out to be in one of the older council estates, not squalid but somehow passed over. Nothing much has changed here since the seventies except that satellite dishes have replaced the Chinese script of TV aerials. Pebble-dash and concrete, brambles of graffiti, a few boarded-up windows. On the green a burned-out car orange with rust with an enormous sofa disembowelled beside it. The Keane house is toward the far end of the innermost terrace, the number I'd jotted down confirmed by the plumber's van parked outside. As I walk toward it, I feel the weight of the anonymous houses watching me.

The front door is answered by a woman in a housecoat. I can hear the thrum of a mower out the back. 'Would Danny be in?'

An emotion, not quite fear, passes over her face. 'Trevor!

Fella here is looking to talk to Danny!' The kitchen door opens and into the hall steps Trevor Keane in shirtsleeves. He replaces his missus at the front door, a big man with a high complexion. We have a nodding acquaintance from the football field. 'I was hoping to have a word with Danny,' I say.

'With Danny, is it? Dan doesn't do any of your subjects.' He shifts, as if caught out on a lie. 'Anyway, he's not here.'

'I expect you've heard, Jamal Shafiq was set upon. Friday evening.' No answer. 'Yes?' He shakes his head, as if he hasn't quite understood me. 'I was at the hospital to see him earlier on.' His face is glazed over. 'He's in a very bad way.'

'What's any of this got to do with Danny?'

'I just thought he might know what Jamal was up to on Friday evening. Who he was with. Why he was in the park…' The sound of the lawnmower dying diverts both of our attentions. He makes a grimace, an exaggeration of dumbness, and says, 'Nah.' Then he breathes in and adds, 'I told you already. He's not here,' and makes to shut the door, but my foot prevents it. His pale eyes are indignant. 'I just need two minutes,' I bid, 'ok?' Before he has the chance to shove the door shut, Danny, in grass-stained tracksuit, appears in the kitchen. There is a jolt when he sees me: a rigidity. In that instant I know that he knows why I'm here.

Over the man's shoulder, I wave. Danny is awkward, unsure whether or how to respond. 'Go upstairs Dan.' He doesn't look at his son; he looks directly at me. Unwilling to put the boy in an impossible position, I wait until Danny has gone upstairs before continuing.

'Mr Keane, I just need to talk to him for two minutes is all.'

'I don't think so.'

'He might know,' I shrug, 'something. Anything. The guards have said that no matter how insignificant…'

'Look. Danny didn't see anything. Danny didn't hear anything. Right? You,' a finger, nicotine yellow, pokes my collarbone, 'leave our boy alone.'

I turn but I remain at the threshold, not yet ready to abandon the hunch I'm working off. 'Let me tell you about brain trauma,' I say. I tell him how my cousin has spent the last twenty years, twisted like a question mark in a wheelchair. 'His life over,' I snap my fingers, 'like that.' He is waiting for me to finish. 'At least that was an accident. He came off a motorbike. But *this*?'

He says something then that takes a second to register. 'You never got married.' There is unguarded loathing pushing up his blood pressure. 'Why is that?'

I guffaw, 'I'm sorry?' But the door has snapped shut on my astonishment. The house is imperturbable, but for a twitch behind the curtain upstairs. A couple of minutes later, as I walk away, the father's voice overtakes me. 'Tough break, your cousin.'

Back in the park, at the footbridge, I'm as jittery as if I've had a thousand coffees. Because there must have been things said in that house. Words exchanged. Maybe even slaps. The first, ugly thought, that it was Trevor Keane who'd landed the boot to the side of Jamal's skull, has gone. Too fantastic. Too…

But there was something *not* being said. Suppose Danny had been with Jamal at the time he was set upon. Suppose he'd left him. Abandoned him. Turned on him. Suppose he knew who'd been behind the attack, and what had motivated it. Should I now go to the guards? Tip them off?

Still I remain, watching the slow flow of the river. Because when it comes to it, what do I know? A gesture, half seen. The wordless menace after a domestic row. A twitch of a curtain. I think of Jamal, lying on the gurney in the thin hospital gown; of the months and years ahead of him. And I think of Andrew, the kiss he pressed on me the night of the crash; and all that I never said to him.

David Butler is a multi-award winning novelist, poet, short story writer and playwright. The most recent of his three published novels, *City of Dis* (New Island) was shortlisted for the Kerry Group Irish Novel of the Year, 2015. His second poetry collection, *All the Barbaric Glass*, was published in March 2017 from Doire Press. Literary prizes include the Maria Edgeworth (twice) and Fish International Award for the short story, the Scottish Community Drama, Cork Arts Theatre and British Theatre Challenge awards for drama, and the Féile Filíochta, Ted McNulty, Brendan Kennelly and Poetry Ireland / Trocaire awards for poetry

SHANNON SAVVAS

Into the Looking Glass

New Zealand, 1965

Yesterday, I didn't know a thirteen-year-old could want to be twelve again. I didn't know you couldn't un-know stuff. I'm not talking fractions or German verbs. I'm talking the understanding tattooed into your brain. Garden of Eden knowledge – now I know what Father McManus was on about at school. He might have been talking rot about evolution not being true, but shame from knowledge, oh God, yes. Not shame from knowing about boys and kissing and ... sex. Babies – heck, I knew since I was eleven – above the waist, no, below the waist, no, no. That's just embarrassing stuff. But shame is something else. The worst of it? It's not my shame etched on the inside wall of my chest where it rubs against my heart and hurt, hurt, hurts.

One birthday. One birthday dinner to be exact.

No going back. Alice got that right. Yesterday you were a different person.

My birthday dinner at El Matador. According to Mother, Auckland's classiest (only for all I knew) restaurant. With waiters and menus and live music and alcohol.

'Can Lindy come?' I asked.

'No.'

'She's my best friend. Please.'

'It's time you chose better friends.'

By better she meant ones who weren't Islanders. Ones who didn't have out-of-work dads and mums who were always pregnant (I'd heard her telling Sister Mary Joseph it might be the Catholic way, but the frequency was unseemly).

'Oh and your Father's boss will be joining us,' she said. 'I expect you to behave, he's American.'

'If he was French would I not have to behave?' A rush of air, a blur but still not fast enough to dodge her clip around my ear.

Three boring adults and me. Great birthday. She'd chosen the swanky restaurant not for me but for the American. Thanks Mother.

Mother. Calling her Carol lasted three months until she read some scathing commentary in the *Auckland Star* about sexually liberal, hippy parents and we were back to Mother. *Mum* and *Dad* were banned. Haughty as the Red Queen, she suited *Mother*. If she could've gotten away with *Mater* and *Pater*, she would've done. But Father, he was a *Dad*.

She swanned into my bedroom, black chiffon glamour, reeking of *Youth Dew* and Benson and Hedges. *Poor – immigrant – Catholic – Irish* that identity was long gone.

'Put these on.' A pair of deflated Siamese snakes, smelling of Persil landed on my bed. Her pantyhose. 'They're more grown-up than socks.'

Pity she hadn't thought about a more grown-up outfit than the dress she'd bought for my twelfth birthday. Lace collar and puffy sleeves, Victorian and embarrassing. It was 1967 not 1867. I was thirteen, for God's sake. Grace Slick was my hero. Even worse, she pinned my hair in a tight bun, she called it a *chignon*, making me all piggy eyes and freckles.

Mother reclined on the sofa in stockinged feet, scintillating in black georgette and imitation diamonds, her black suede stilettos with mink pompoms collapsed on the carpet like tired kittens. I coveted those shoes, wanted her lipsticks and desired her nail polishes. Sometimes I wished she'd die.

Father kept glancing at his watch, fingering his clip-on bow tie and checking his wallet. Awkward but gorgeous. Dagwood Bumstead to Mother's Blondie.

'For God's sake. Lewis.' She held out her glass.

'You look gorgeous, Carol.' Pride and love papered his face.

'Just pour me another gin.'

One sip of his refill and she slammed the glass down. 'Did you forget the gin?' she said.

Saved by the doorbell, Father went to answer the door while Mother scrambled into her shoes, putting her anger back on its leash.

A very American Mr Burke, with his crew cut and big smile filled our living room.

'Stoney, this is Carol, and this is my birthday girl, Alicia.'

He took Mother's hand. 'It's really Max, but most people call me Stoney.'

'Stoney, it is then.' She blasted him with her Lauren Hutton gap-tooth smile. Someone must have told her (probably Father) that it was cute. Whoever, she believed it.

It must have been too much because he turned to me.

'Well, you sure are a beautiful thirteen-year-old, Alicia.' All he needed was a white Stetson.

My skin fizzled with pleasure. Prairie fires raced up, down, around my body. I had shifted from kid to grown up.

Stoney's free hand held two corsages, purple orchids tied with white satin ribbon.

'The occasion demanded something special,' he said. 'But you girls make the orchids look ordinary.'

He looked at me when he said it. He did.

'You Americans are always so gallant,' Mother said. Vivien Leigh could have taken lessons in simper and drawl.

'Shall I pin it for you, Carol?' Father asked.

She turned her back on him and his stupid grin froze on his face. She offered Stoney the corsage. 'Stoney will do it. Go start the car Lewis or we'll be late.'

Stoney pinned the flowers above her heart. 'Now what about you, young lady?'

'I'll do it,' Mother said. 'She's shy. You'll make her blush again.'

El Matador, shadowy stairs up to a darkened room crowded with oases of rosy lamplight. Wine red walls, posters of matadors in tight scarlet trousers and black ballet pumps flourished blood-red capes and taunted monstrous black bulls. Waiters glided between tables, crockery clinked and private conversations syncopated with a lazy trickle of jazz.

A scowl dressed like Fred Astaire in black tie and tails asked if we had a reservation.

'Carpenter, party of four? I booked last week?' Father sounded like a man pleading for a bank loan.

Wet lips pursed and one eyebrow lifted. What was his problem? We weren't wearing gumboots. Father fiddled with his bowtie and cleared his throat while the bloke ran his finger down an unseen list.

Felt like waiting for confession when crabby Father Delaney was in the box. I hung back expecting the Maître D' to tell Father there was no reservation for the likes of us.

'Your table is in the annex. Someone will show you the way.' Whew.

Stoney stepped up. 'I wonder,' he said, taking out his wallet, 'would you have a better table nearer the music?'

Eyes flickered at the twenty rolled like a cigar. 'Of course, Sir. Let me see what I can do, Sir. This way, Sir.'

A table near the dance floor. Stoney gave Fred the money.

'Merci, Monsieur.'

Weirdo, speaking French. Shouldn't it have been, *gracias, Senor*?

'Look and learn, Lewis,' Mother whispered to Father. 'Look and learn.'

I looked and learned.

Father took what he got given.

Stoney took what he wanted.

Hairline fissures zigzagged under my feet.

This was another world. I'd stepped into an episode of *I Love Lucy*. Pink linen water lilies sat on the fuchsia tablecloths and gleaming silver lay in formation at each setting. Cartoon tendrils of sweet cigar smoke teased my nose and a bottle opened with a loud sucking pop at the next table. Real champagne bubbled into glasses. Just like the movies. Swank and sophisticated. Grown up.

A waiter, ratfaced, with pimples, held my chair and smirked. Should I sit or stand and wait for him to shove it into my knees? I looked at Mother.

'For heaven's sake, Alicia, sit down.'

I sat, he pushed the chair and my bottom hit the seat at just the right moment. Then the idiot flicked my napkin, ruining the water lily. I reached to take it just as his hands fumbled it into my lap. My hand bounced off his skin, and knocked the cutlery to the floor. Everyone around stopped talking and looked. Stoney smiled. Mother gave me her evil eye and Father bent to pick up the silverware. I prayed the pink lights would camouflage the red tide flooding my stupid face.

Mother dropped her clutch on the table and removed her elbow length gloves. Stoney suggested whiskey sours and Mother ordered a Coke for me after the waiter handed us leather menus.

A Nancy Sinatra lookalike in white knee-high boots, an amazing silver mini-dress and backcombed blond hair joined the band. She sang *The Green, Green Grass of Home*. Her voice wasn't as good as Nancy's, though. A few old couples danced.

I couldn't imagine dancing in the arms of a Hollywood man like Stoney. But I tried.

'Are you ready to order, ladies and gentlemen?' Ratface asked in a hokey French accent.

Father looked as if the choice was hanging or drowning. Stoney suggested champagne and Bluff oysters to start.

'Wonderful,' Mother said. She laid her hand on his arm. 'So nice when a man knows what he wants.'

The fissures split into cracks.

Father's eyes swung over the prices and ordered shrimp cocktail for him and me.

'And the main dish for you, *Mademoiselle*'? Ratface smarmed over my shoulder. His breath smelt of stale cigarettes and beer. If he thought his smirk was charming, I thought it was creepy. Mother jumped in and ordered for me.

'She will have the chicken-in-the-basket.' She informed everyone, 'I read Queen Elizabeth eats chicken with her hands, so that'll make it easier for Alicia.'

I wanted to slide under the table. Did the Queen eat with her hands, did she? Did Mother think I was a baby? I was thirteen. Couldn't she let me choose something for myself? Father ordered the same, saying it reminded him of his Navy days in Boston.

'And the lovely Molly you tell us you were engaged to?' Mother said.

Father laughed his cheesy laugh and shook his head.

Stoney ordered a blue steak. It sounded exotic and I wished I were having it too.

'That sounds marvellous,' said Mother. 'I'll have the same.'

The oysters were disgusting grey globules of snot. Mother said she was allergic to shellfish, her glance daring Father to deny it.

When I asked if I could try some champagne, Mother said no and gave me her behave- yourself-look before turning back to Stoney.

'Why not, Carol, it's her birthday,' Stoney said pouring me a glass. 'She's growing up.'

'It's not sweet. She won't like it,' Mother said. The skin above her Betty Boop lips blanched.

But I did like it.

Stoney lit her cigarette and filled her glass.

'I can't see the band,' she said shuffling her chair closer to him. 'Now that's what I call a better view.'

Fissures became cracks.

Father sipped his drink and smoked.

Stoney's steak, swimming in bloody juices, streaked his napkin like a sanitary towel whenever he dabbed his mouth. Mother barely touched her bleeding lump of meat, prodding it with her fork as if she expected it to get up and trot off. I managed only half my chicken, with my knife and fork. Father finished his and swapped plates with me.

'Forget dessert,' she said when Ratty cleared the plates. 'You're obviously not hungry.'

The band played *Begin the Beguine*.

'Oh, I love this,' she said, 'but Lewis can't dance to save his life. Or mine. I didn't find out until our wedding reception. He marched me up and down as if he was on a parade ground.' She winked at Stoney, her eyes glinting like *Woolworths'* tinsel.

'Lewis, may I dance with Carol?'

'Sure, she'd love that.'

Stoney was a good dancer, despite Mother dancing too close to him. I hoped he wouldn't ask me to dance. That would be worse than when Mother made me dance with her at family parties. Even worse would be if he didn't ask me.

Stoney's hand cabbed across Mother's back before sidling down to the top of her bum.

The cracks gaped wider.

Father fiddled with his cufflinks. Whew. He hadn't noticed.

Mr Burke and Mother danced to *Can't Take My Eyes Off You* and Father lit one cigarette after another, tumbling his birthday

Ronson lighter over and over between his fingers. Mother mouthed the words to *Strangers in the Night* against Mr Burke's neck while he rested his American cheek on her brow.

'Wish I danced.' Father reached for another cigarette. 'Want to dance, sweetheart?'

I shook my head. God no.

The American lowered his head and whispered in Mother's ear. She laughed. When the song finished they threaded their way back to the table. Mr Burke loomed large and out of place. I wouldn't have danced with him if he asked me. Mother stopped and whispered to a waiter. Perhaps she wanted the toilet. I know I did. I wanted a wee and my head was fuzzy. She sat down, raised her eyebrows and nodded to Mr Burke.

The cracks became chasms.

The band stumbled to silence.

The maître D' laid a cake covered in tumbling, pink sugar-roses before me. The whole restaurant sang *Happy Birthday.* My face burnt fiercer than the thirteen candles.

The cake glued my tongue to the roof of my mouth.

'Lewis, Alicia's tired, drive her home,' Mother said. 'I'll take a taxi when the band wraps up. Stoney will keep me company.' She flashed him her lighthouse smile. 'And Lewis, don't wait up.'

The ground crumbled and I tumbled like Alice into a deep hole.

A New Zealand writer living in Cyprus, **Shannon Savvas** has had one story called The Loneliness of the Long-Distance Woman, published in Headland's inaugural issue, January 2015, was short-listed in the Page & Blackmore short story competition 2017 and long-listed in the Bath Flash Fiction competition, 2017. She has failed miserably at writing her novel, re-writes in double figures, but lives with hope.

JUDITH WILSON

Hunger in the Air

Emma raises the knife.

'Cake?'

'No, not that much.' Sasha flutters her hand to the right, slicing minutely.

'You *bought* it?' Christa's eyes are on Emma, cool as flint.

Anna says nothing. It's always the same.

The women are silent. 'My girls!' That's what their mother liked to say. Emma knows Anna will have the last word.

'Carrot?' Anna stares. 'Why not lemon? Or chocolate? Mum *hated* carrot.'

'I wasn't thinking. It was the first one I saw.' Emma stares at the sugar decoration. It blurs before her eyes. Stupid, no, she didn't think.

The four women sit in perfect quarters around the table; their alignment is uncanny. On the glossy mahogany there's a roll of embroidered fabric, tied tight. Emma's knife, it's still hovering. In truth, she has no stomach for sweetness. None of them do. Outside the winter sun has slipped away.

Emma puts down the knife, touches the silk roll.

'I don't believe it,' Christa's glance hardens. 'You've *looked* already?'

'No! I only just found it.' Emma. Eldest. *Magpie, more like*. She knows they're all thinking it. But she's merely taking charge.

'I want the ruby ring.' Anna. She has no shame.

Out loud Emma says:'I thought mum made notes, who was to have what. I couldn't find them?'

It's an invitation for comment and the sisters rise to it, speaking at once, four heads bobbing, hair from caramel to raven, Emma's grey carefully disguised.

'I looked in the desk.'

'In her underwear drawer.'

'They'll be here somewhere.'

Of course they've hunted. Emma knows that. Each of them popping back to their mother's flat at odd times in those final weeks, they all have a key. Departing the hospital, to 'check things are okay, are the windows locked?' Leaving her bedside 'to breathe fresh air, wash my face.' Each sister standing alone these desolate days amongst their mother's possessions, half an eye on what might soon 'be mine', a careful hand here, a cautious arm there. Despite the early rise of grief, barely warm, ebbing slow. Despite their mother, bravely preparing for death.

Emma knows her sisters have hunted; she's hunted herself.

It was only yesterday afternoon when her mother announced, *sotto voce*, where to find the parcel. Just the two of them together – like old times.

Sasha pushes away her cake, pours tea. She knows without asking who takes what. One lemon slice for Anna, milk for Emma; Christa has two sugars. She fills her own mug from the kettle. She dunks a herbal teabag, swirls it, water ginger-pale.

'Go on then, take a look.' Christa leans forward, eager.

They all want the ruby ring.

Eight hands flutter towards the parcel, but Anna fingers it first.

The familiar cracked leather box sits like a queen amongst the costume pieces. They're pretty enough: enameled earrings, a pearl necklace and the aquamarine pendant. The Forties watch, crocodile-strapped, they remember it well.

But they all want the ring.

Emma ought to have it. First-born. Mum's favourite. She's forged the career her mother had to abandon back in the Sixties, when women bred, rather than worked. Her eldest daughter 'Called to the Bar', she'd puff out her chest saying it. Emma has climbed the career ladder, garnered respect in a city firm. She has two handsome sons also bound for the law. Mum has always spoken of her with swelling pride.

'My eldest daughter, she's in the legal profession. Did I say?'

But that's not why Emma needs the ruby. Now she shuts her eyes, summons a memory, quite visceral. Her mother, heavy with ripened stomach in a cotton smock, telling her: 'I've a baby coming! A present for you!'

'I don't want to share!'

Little Emma couldn't bear her mother split in two, didn't want a rival. *'Bad baby!'* She'd screamed it often, puce with jealousy. But that faded afternoon, there was only the comforting twinkle of the ring on her mother's puffy hand. She'd kissed Emma's tiny palm with fluttery lips. 'You'll always be special. My best girl.'

Emma wants the ruby ring as a reminder of her mother's love.

She wants it very much.

But Sasha also desires it. Not for herself long-term, oh no!

'I'll give it to Melissa. Pass it down the generations.'

She's always thought it, said it on repeat over the years.

'After all, I'm the only one with a *daughter*.'

The air crackles as Sasha intones it. As if on cue, Melissa sweeps in from outside, her parka hood up. She's eighteen:

long-legged and golden-faced, they all love her, the aunts, of course they do. But female jealousy, it's a funny thing. They adore Melissa's bright freedom and the promise of her future; they know theirs is already half-bitten. They see her strong resemblance to their mother; recognize her pure spirit, alternative and daring.

But they hate her for it too; just a tiny bit.

'Melissa – you'd really want a *ring*?' Christa asks it. She views Melissa's string bracelets, that crucifix, her typical rag-tag teenage displays.

Melissa halts halfway across the sitting room. Her face is splashed with rain, in her hands, carrier bags squeezed with the contents of her grandmother's hospital locker. She'd offered to drive home Sasha's car after the death. Neither her mother, nor the aunts, had known what to do. While they wept, one in the passenger seat, a tight threesome at the back, Melissa had put her own grief on hold. She'd loved her grandmother, knew she was a kindred spirit. Now she sees the cake, she's hungry and she wants a slice. No one has offered.

Then she spots the ring box. Immediately cancels her desire.

'It's between all of you,' she says. 'You need to decide.'

She disappears into her grandmother's bedroom, inhales her powdery scent. These four daughters, they don't see the teenage girl collapse on the bed, bury her face in her grandmother's eiderdown.

Melissa knows it's only a matter of time.

Sasha regards her own tapered fingers, tries to ignore the few age spots spreading on her tanned skin. They're already bejeweled: a sapphire cluster, the matching platinum wedding ring, and a fancy diamond eternity band. This one presented soon after Melissa arrived. David, he's generous with his gifts. If only he wasn't so expansive with his largesse amongst others. *Other women*. If only …

Christa breaks the silence. She must confess, the carrot cake slipped down a treat. She hasn't eaten properly in days, is abruptly starving. (Perhaps she's lost a pound or two, with the stress and all.) She thinks of Buster and Furnace pining for her company back home. Pictures Alan, manfully popping in to walk them – on the same heath where they met three years ago. Christa recalls Alan's desperate embrace the occasional nights he stays over. She wonders if he'll *ever* leave his wife?

She rests a palm on the ripple of her midriff. If she had the ring, seeing it might jolt him into asking her to marry him and he'd leave his wife.

Would it? *Could it?*

'Mother said I should have the ruby.'

Three pairs of eyes swivel, so Christa blurts it out now.

'I'm unmarried. You've all got beautiful rings. *I* should have it.'

'Bullshit.' Anna's mouth is a tiny full stop.

'Come on Christa.' Emma doesn't want to be unkind. But Christa always plays this trump card. Of course they feel bad for her. The broken engagement years before, the wedding insurance cashed, *that look* on their father's face. Three redundant bridesmaids, those yards of wasted lilac silk.

Christa's tears flood her powdered cheeks.

'Oh don't, sis!'

Sasha knows that if Christa cries, they'll all weep, a cacophony of fear and isolation, pent-up emotion after these weeks of distress. For the mother they've lost, who loved each daughter in her own special way.

Emma cuts Christa more cake. 'There's cream cheese frosting.'

Anna snorts out loud.

'Chocolate – now *that* was mother's favourite.' She sweeps her gaze around the room. Her plate is still empty. She's defiant.

'I want the ruby ring. You lot can divide everything else.'

Anna, the youngest, a late mistake and loved too much.

Anna – a warm and milky baby, cradled in her mother's hungry embrace, whilst her three elders ascended the ranks at school. Winning academic prizes (Emma), sports trophies (Sasha), Domestic Science (Christa). Anna, the baby everyone indulged. Anna, who read adult books so early, won a place to Cambridge, aged barely 17.

Anna, who dropped out one year later, never went back.

Anna, married too young, aborted a baby, disappeared, ignoring her mother's total distress. She'd returned separated and unrepentant.

She doesn't deserve that ruby ring. The sisters are silent in unison.

Now Anna leans forward, confident in her claim.

'Ruby is the birthstone for July. My birthday.'

Her fingers close on the box. The sisters hold their breath. Anna opens it.

The ruby ring, though. *It's gone.*

Melissa hears them arguing one full hour. The sisters hurl abuse and accusations. There are tears. A plate breaks. Eventually, silence. When she joins them, knowing she must, her grandmother's jewellery is laid out, glittering necklaces and baubles. The granddaughter's heart thumps; early grief pushes in. Her mother, the three aunts: their faces are swollen with leftover anger. They've divided everything into neat piles. Sasha looks up.

'I've saved you a brooch. That's all.'

Melissa sits. As a child, with her grandmother she'd often look at the ruby ring; she'd count its four diamonds, two either side of the scarlet gemstone, touching them reverently with a chubby finger, weaving private fairytales.

Emma stands. She's all wrung out, but swirling in her stomach is the tiniest thread of hope, the chance of repair. 'Hot chocolate?' she asks.

Her sisters, eyes red-rimmed, look up. They're ashamed, they've made a mess; their mother would not have approved.

But whenever there was a fight at home, she'd always say: 'Hot chocolate?'

Now Emma takes on mum's role. In the kitchen, she finds the tin. It's almost empty. She hopes there will be enough, shakes it, opens up.

'What the hell?'

The tin is clean. Inside it, four white envelopes are labeled Emma, Sasha, Christa and Anna. A note:

'*You were all so different. So: a different style for each.*'

Emma's hands are shaking as she doles the envelopes.

They open them. For Emma, a delicate chain, the diamond at its tip. For Sasha: a diamond bracelet. For Christa, a brooch, the diamond inside a silver flower. For Anna, a gold coin, the diamond nestled at its core.

'She's split the ring!' Anna's hands fasten her pendant. 'Where's the ruby?'

She snatches the note. On the rear, in her mother's handwriting, dated one month before. Long before her illness dive-bombed: '*You'd argue over it,*' she'd written. '*I hope you'll understand.*'

Mother, she was always unconventional. And Melissa, she's her natural successor. The four daughters know that. Now Emma gets up, draws Melissa to the table. There was no envelope for her. They've all noticed.

'We do love you.' Emma holds Melissa's hand. 'You know that?'

The sisters regard her carefully. Melissa's heart leaps against her ribs. It's now or never. She twists her hair into a ponytail, doesn't know how to break the news. She fixes a hair elastic, holds still. There's a new gold stud in her right earlobe, set with a sparkling ruby.

'She wanted to. I didn't ask.' Melissa gazes at them. 'I'm sorry.'

The four women sit in silence. They're all wondering what to say – if there *is* anything to say. But no, there's nothing to forgive.

Mother wanted this. They all think it. Know it. They understand.

Melissa disappears into the kitchen, makes tea. No one moves. When she returns, they all look with impeccable timing at the carrot cake. The cream cheese frosting, it's glistening. Melissa tosses her ponytail. Around the table, four diamonds and one ruby twinkle. It's as if nothing has happened at all.

The four daughters smile at Melissa, lean forward. So does she.

Now there's hunger in the air.

'Cake?' Emma asks.

And she raises the knife.

Judith Wilson is a writer and journalist. She has won the Retreat West Short Story Prize 2016 and 2nd prize for the inaugural Colm Toibin International Short Story Award 2016; her stories have been long-listed for the Ink Tears Short Story Contest 2016 and commended for the Cinnamon Press Annual Short Story Prize 2016. Judith is also the author of 14 non-fiction books on interiors. She's a Faber Academy Alumna and is putting the finishing touches to her first novel. When not in London, she'll usually be found in Cornwall, close to the sea. www.judithwilsonwrites.com

JOE EURELL

Little Comrade

I'm lying in bed when there's a knock at the door. But I can't sleep anyway shivering under the threadbare sheet mother has bound around me, with the tick of the grandfather clock coming from the hall. I pull an old sweater over my pyjamas and wander to the top of the stairs. She beats me to the door and darkness floods the hallway, almost as if it comes from the shadow towering over her.

'Mrs Rusev?' he says, stepping inside without an invite. 'Major Danchev. We spoke on the telephone.' He follows the light from the front room and stomps his boots as he goes, leaving clumps of snow behind. Mother says nothing when if that was me I'd be on my hands and knees.

I hear him talking to my brother, Nikolaj, while she frets in the kitchen. It means I'm the only one left out, having been sent to bed like a child. The kettle hisses and mother returns with tea. I shuffle down a few stairs on my bottom and watch through the banister rails.

'It's only Nettle,' she says. 'We don't have many visitors.'

Major Danchev takes a steaming cup and sits in father's armchair. I try not to hold it against him. The fire casts his pockmarked face orange as he risks a sip. I've tasted mother's tea and it's not a risk worth taking.

'It's fine,' he says. 'Only I take mine a little stronger.' He pulls a bottle from his pocket and pours a splash into his cup, before putting the rakia on the table. Its sticky sweet contents trickle down the side of the bottle and stain the label brown. 'Care for some, Nikolaj? Since the bottle's yours.'

Mother glares at my brother but amongst the fire and the tea and the rakia the atmosphere is the only frosty thing in the room, and I want to be downstairs too. I huddle into my sweater and wait for Major Danchev to reveal why he's really here. A man of his rank wouldn't concern himself with a minor drinking.

He's in no rush to face the cold and leans back into the chair, with its worn fabric on the headrest and burn marks from father's pipe. He asks for another tea and boasts to Nikolaj about his time at the front, tapping the row of medals pinned to his barrel-shaped chest.

When mother returns I can see from above that her roots are grey. We must be out of boot polish.

'My father used to have a saying,' Nikolaj says, breaking his silence. 'The more medals on a man's chest, the less action he's seen.'

Major Danchev arches an eyebrow. His only one since they meet in the middle.

'I'll overlook your smart mouth but not your age. The policeman who stopped you documented it as seventeen, yet our records show you served two years ago.'

Nikolaj's smart mouth stops smirking. It was father's idea of patriotism, having him enlist underage.

Mother shows Major Danchev out. There wasn't much to talk about once it's clear Nikolaj's national service is void and he must re-enlist. I scramble upstairs but the night air still claws at me when she opens the door. Major Danchev feels it too and braces himself against the cold by turning up his collar.

'Before I go, Mrs Rusev, our records also show you have another son.'

'That's right. My Georgi turns fifteen soon.'

Major Danchev looks up the stairs, right at me.

'Then I'll be back for you in a year, little Comrade.'

Mother slams the door and after all Nikolaj has done, the glare she reserves for me is worse.

'What have I told you about eavesdropping?' she says. 'And take off your father's sweater.'

The next day Nikolaj takes me with him to the slopes. But the only money in town comes from the mountains so that's where everybody else goes too. We hit traffic and as the Lada struggles uphill the radio is drowned out by the pound of the snow chains.

Nikolaj stops the car. Not that it matters. We're practically at a stop anyway.

'One of the chains is loose,' he says, pointing to the passenger side like that makes it my problem. I shouldn't even be here. It's not my fault he can't manage without Father.

He takes my huffing as a hint and gets out himself. I turn up the heater and watch it eat away at the condensation on the window screen, revealing the snow topped peaks in the distance. It kicks up dirty air, making me cough. I'll not complain though. It's the only time I'll feel warm all day.

Sure enough, when we arrive at the cabin the cold pinches my ears. The shutters whistle with rust as Nikolaj pulls them open and I go to the equipment shed before he can have the satisfaction of telling me to. As I struggle for breath lugging boots and helmets and skis taller than I am, ready for the tourists to rent from us, he's already sneaking off. There's been a fresh flurry overnight and I follow his footprints to see him leaving the cabin. Leaving me to do the work.

We're not doing much business, which means at least the chalet bar did last night. My only customer is a child with excitement in his eyes and crumpled roubles in his mittened hands. I hand him some goggles and Nikolaj breezes back in holding coffee and a half eaten cruller. My stomach squirms at the smell but there's nothing for me.

As their hangovers fade the tourists form a queue at the cabin. An older man pushes his way to the front and slaps his briefcase on the counter. The sun glints off his milk bottle lenses and Nikolaj laughs at the idea of this relic going down the red run. But it's clear he's no tourist, everyone else in line with their fair hair and blue eyes and teeth as white as the snow beneath them.

'Nikolaj Rusev? I'm Doctor Anoshkin. Here for your physical.'

They disappear, leaving me to deal with the rush. I struggle to get the queue any shorter and know they're complaining. Cursing sounds the same in any language.

The next customer is unusually tall and stoops under our sign to get to the counter. He asks for boots in a twelve and I spray a pair with disinfectant. The canister says *pine fresh* but smells nothing like the Norwegian Spruces that line the trail. The chemicals get into my cracked skin and it feels like a bee has stung me between the knuckles. I hide my annoyance while he has no such issues, pouting when he can't cram his feet inside the boots. He's no more a size twelve than I am.

'Wait there,' I say. 'We might have something out back.' I race to the equipment shed, being careful of the black ice on the path where the salt has only done half its job. Just like Nikolaj who should have helped me stock the cabin properly this morning. The Baltic winds have warped the wood and I struggle to get the shed door open. With an extra hard tug it comes free and there's Nikolaj, sitting on a box with his trousers around his ankles. His legs are covered in dark hair which stands on end thanks to the draft I've bought in with me.

Dr Anoshkin holds a hammer which he taps my brother with under the knee. Nikolaj is too busy screaming at me to notice. At least he curses in Russian.

Dr Anoshkin returns to the cabin and tells me not to worry about interrupting.

'A strange place to conduct a physical,' he says. 'Your mother was quite insistent he didn't miss work.' I can imagine that conversation. Travelling forty kilometres from town to the mountains being easier than saying no to a woman like her. Yet if Nikolaj passes his medical it's a journey I'll be taking more often. Mother has her own job and it will fall to me to keep the cabin open.

'It's a shame his patellar reflex is so bad. His leg hardly moved,' I say.

Dr Anoshkin smiles at someone showing an interest in his craft and opens his briefcase. He shows me his reflex hammer and his stethoscope and his tongue depressors, which are spotted with rust from a thousand mouths. When I finish school I want to be a doctor. Or a lawyer. Or anything that takes me far away from here.

Once I've finished looking, he returns the depressors to his case and they chink against the glass vials inside.

'I know you don't want him to go,' he says, and I blush at being so transparent. 'But it's normal to miss your brother and a fit, young man like him will sail through basic training.' I turn to carry on with my work when Dr Anoshkin reaches over the counter and there's a cold, sharp sensation at my chest. He puts the other end of his stethoscope in his ear and listens to my breath crackle. 'Your asthma though. It might be a different story come your turn.'

Mother hands me my lunch while I wait for the school bus at the curb. I don't need to look inside to know I'll regret it. The smell of beetroot permeates the paper bag. She thinks if I eat enough vegetables then nothing bad will happen to me like it did to father. It's more likely to happen to her standing outside in her dressing gown.

'Go inside, mother,' I say. 'Or you'll be the one needing the borsch.'

But she won't. Because after I get on the bus another one will come for Nikolaj and neither of us will see him for a year.

'Georgi's leaving,' she shouts at the open door. 'Come say goodbye to your brother!'

She's wasting her breath. I won't waste mine as I don't have it to spare. Nikolaj came in drunk last night and I had to help him onto the top bunk, where he tossed and turned until my alarm went off. Mother's shivering so I walk her inside, turning too late to see the bus go past with my classmates grinning and waving inside.

By the time I've walked to school the hems of my trousers are soaking and if my feet weren't numb I'd feel that my socks are too. I've missed first period and am about to miss second, having been sent to Headmaster Ivanov to explain my tardiness.

He keeps me waiting but I know he's in his office. I can hear his voice boom down the telephone. I can see his shadow through the frosted glass. There's nothing to do but to stare at the flag pinned to the wall opposite. Its colourful stripes stir nothing more in me than the sickle and star that came before them.

My breathing's still heavy from the walk and I search my backpack for my inhaler. I take out my textbooks and my pencil-case and the borsch and feel the panic rising as I remember puffing on it after hauling all six-foot two of Nikolaj into bed and leaving it under my pillow. I tip the rest of my backpack out, even though I know it's not there, and drop to my knees when the inhaler appears in front of my face.

I look up and it's Nikolaj holding it.

In his uniform he looks every inch the soldier. His detour

will make him late to enlist though and we both know his punishment will be far greater than a dressing down from headmaster.

'I spoke to Uncle Stanis. He'll look after the cabin when I'm away.'

'Uncle Stanis is a drunk,' I say, taking a puff on my inhaler. I feel my lungs loosen up and wish I could do the same.

'A drunk who's keeping you in school.' Nikolaj smirks and for once I don't mind at all.

The door opens and the headmaster stands before us.

'What's going on here?' he says, thrown by the soldier standing next to me.

'I was just commending your student,' Nikolaj says, as I stuff my things into my backpack. 'One of my snow chains came loose coming into Stadtvoch and he insisted on helping. It made Comrade Rusev here miss his bus so I wanted to come and thank him properly.'

The headmaster eyes us both but there's no resemblance. Nikolaj has a body beyond his years, tall and broad like Grandfather Orlov, whereas I am short and slight. A Rusev through and through.

'And you are?' he says.

'Major Danchev,' Nikolaj says, and the headmaster's face softens like the snow come June.

He promises an honourable mention for the school and I'm excused back to class so the grownups can carry on their conversation.

I walk away and it occurs to me for the first time that I might actually miss my brother. A year will go quickly, I tell myself. But not too quickly, I hope, knowing that when it does the real Major Danchev will be back for his little Comrade.

Joe Eurell is a writer from Birmingham who is currently editing his first novel (a process he fears will never end). In between drafts he enjoys writing shorter fiction to cleanse his palate. One of these stories has recently been shortlisted for the Bath Flash Fiction Award, and his work has been published in print, online and broadcast media. To find out more about Joe and his writing, follow him on Twitter @JoeEurell

COLIN WALSH

Seen/Unseen

They've used a wiry piece of twine to bind her hands together in a gesture of supplication. She looks as though she's lying in the box waiting for communion. Her face is shrunken, not at all like she's sleeping, despite what some of these sentimental old fucks are nodding to one another. Her eyes are closed, of course. Though I've seen dead eyes before. They're all depth without profundity. Indifferent reflectors. They never bother me. Still, I wouldn't want to see such glassy voids in the skull of my own mother. I'm not a complete monster, underneath it all, blah blah blah.

The mourners coming and going like a conveyor belt.

Sorry for your loss.

She was a great woman.

Oh she'll be missed.

She is at peace now.

She isn't suffering where she is now.

She's looking down on you now.

That's the end of an era now.

It's like being in a factory. Mechanically reaching out and shaking hands, till they shuffle on with the heads bowed, clutching beads. Will you come back to the house tomorrow, after the burial? I say, like a reflex. I've said it so many times the phrase is acquiring its own melody. Like a fucking ring-tone. Will you come back to the house tomorrow, after the burial? I give them an understanding nod before they get their excuses out. Soft cunts.

It's awkward, of course. Plenty of these people despise me. Fear me, even. Sure, they're shaking my hand, but that's not for me. It's out of respect for tradition, for her; a final gesture, a reaching out to something lost. Many of them can't even look at me. Never did look at me. Never will again, after today, I suppose. They'll be long dead by the time I'm out again.

First they shake my hand then they shake the hand of Garda Byrne. They can look at him easy enough. Not a bother. They smile at him. Some even thank him, the prick.

Ach, he's not the worst.

It's a terrible business, he said to me in the car when we left the prison. Losing a parent, like. You never get over it, really.

Some people would say things like that only trying to get under your skin, but I knew that wasn't Byrne's way. That's why he gets assigned to these things. The compassionate sort. Helped me fix the disaster I made of my black tie. Asked if I wanted a cuppa, more than once. Looked away when I was feeling low. He seems the type you could have a pint with.

There'll be no pints. Not allowed for me, along with everything else. Compassionate release, or whatever the fuck… Very little of either for me in this room. Compassion or release. Just candles, a coffin and an orderly queue. Classical music in the background, mother of jesus.

I haven't been to a viewing or a funeral in years, obviously. Never been the mourner-in-chief either. Haven't a notion what to actually do. Just keep shaking the hands. Will you come back to the house tomorrow, after the burial? I say.

Whole thing costs a bloody fortune. She paid for it herself.

The death certificate was also taken care of without me. Turns out my mother was an organ donor. Turns out she knew where she wanted to be buried, and had reserved the plot. Was on first name terms with the funeral director, Simmons. Gave clear instructions. Always organized. And she'd decided on the readings; one for me, and a couple for the bridge club ladies. Eulogy to be delivered by the priest himself, who seems a decent sort. Young fella. Offered me a smoke when me and Byrne first arrived. Knew her well, apparently.

Byrne had been chatting to me in the car about the need to cancel everything to do with standing orders, coal deliveries, bin collections, TV license, unpaid bills. I barely heard him. The sensation of being in a moving car, the world opening on all sides of me, was already a bit much.

Turned out she had organized all that shit anyway.

She wanted The Moody Blues tune 'Go Now' played at the burial. I could only imagine the faces. Mammy was always good for a laugh. Would've hated all this solemnity. The bowed heads, the whispers, all the bullshit pouring out their mouths.

Wasn't she awful brave.

She'd a tough auld run.

She was a saint.

And I only talking to her the other morning.

Sure she was a demon for the fags.

She'd never leave you gasping for a cuppa.

Oh she was a mighty woman altogether.

I wish they'd all just fuck off. She was my mother. Mine. What do they actually know of her, with their sympathies and their fucking lemon drizzle cakes? Do they know about the time when Mr. Mannion accused me of breaking the window with a football and she marched into the school to take the head off him? Led him out into the school yard demanding to see the broken window? Mocked him when he showed her a window that had already been fixed? Demanded an apology?

Demanded he address his apologies to me, six-year-old me? And when Mannion protested and instructed me to show my mother how the window had been broken, and I picked up a ball and kicked it through the new pane of glass, how she laughed at his dismayed puss and said serves you right you toe-rag and giggled with her arm around me all the way home?

They don't know any of it.

Joyless fucks. They'll never know how she used to look at me. They're just here for a gawk at the fuck-up son who never knew how sick she was. These fuckers milling about. All so desperate to look at me but they avoid my eye, the way nervous dogs do. Shit-the-bed dogs. Every now and then I pick a gawker out of the crowd and stare them down. These cunts wilt and wither the moment you clock your lamps on them.

None of them deserve to be here. My mother deserved better than this.

They keep on coming.

I'd murder a drink. You'd murder a lot of things, I hear Mam say. Ha ha. For fuck's sake.

The whole shaking hands thing seems to be dying down now. A strange stillness in the air.

My mother in a box.

Byrne catches my eye and gives a sympathetic sort of nod. Ah, jesus.

Some auld fella with a head like a burst arsehole pipes up, shall we say a prayer?

He looks at me when he says it, and the room suddenly funnels down upon me. Avalanching. I look at the floor and shrug, yeah go on.

They all gather closer to the coffin. When no one says anything, I realise they're all looking at me again. There's some awkward throat-clearing. Ah, now. They want me to lead a call and response. I can barely remember the fucking Hail Mary, never mind anything else. I knew the Hail Mary when I was about four, like. I remember sitting with some other kid by the radiator in playschool, giddy as we shouted 'of thy womb, *jaysus*', 'of thy womb, *jaysus*' at one another. One of the childminders tore us apart, sent me to stand in the corner, face to the wall. The wall was bright red brick. I could feel everyone's eyes on my back.

I can feel their eyes all over me now, too, next to my mother in a box.

Ah, jesus.

Byrne steps up to end my misery; the Angel of the Lord declared unto Mary…

I mouth the words along with him and the crowd join in. My face is flushing redbrick red. I bow so no one will see, but they must know. Cunts. Their voices swell and fill my head. They can't even recite the prayer in sync, it all just sounds like gibbering, like the murmurs of someone in a nightmare. But Mam isn't having a nightmare. She's horizontal and her eyes are closed because she's dead. My mother is dead. This is a fucking disgrace. These people are a disgrace.

The room's fallen silent again. Byrne leans in. They're wondering, he says, if it might be time to close the coffin.

I don't say anything. I just shake my head. Shake my head like, no, it's not time. Or, no, please don't.

Who wants to say a rosary, I say.

Burst Arsehole licks his chops, ready to launch into it, but Byrne steps in again. Good man. I believe in one God, the Father, the Almighty, maker of heaven and earth, of all things seen and unseen, I believe and on and on.

Everyone looks serious. Heads bowed, even though she wasn't their mother. Even though she was mine.

The rosary goes on for ages. Some belt it out, others allow the words to slither over their lips in airy half-articulations. I'm moving my mouth but I don't know the right words. And I know they want to close my mother up in a coffin now. They're just waiting for the end of the prayer.

When the silence falls again, it is different. Charged.

Glances flit back and forth. Nobody moves. They're waiting for me.

I take a step to the coffin. My heart's leaping all about the room. It feels like the room is expanding and contracting. Like I am wading in a great big heart that's pumping something ferocious. I stand over the coffin. I can hear myself breathing. My chest going in, out. It's loud. Sort of ragged.

My mother. Mammy.

I bow to kiss her, when suddenly she jerks her hands apart. She holds them out like Christ, like Mary, like someone pleading. They're talons. Curled claws.

People scream. Holy Mary mother of God! They fall back. Men shout.

Mother of fuck! I say. Mother of fuck!

It takes a couple of seconds for me to realise that the twine holding her hands together has snapped, that she hasn't done a Lazarus, it's just the rigor mortis. People bless themselves frantically, trying to catch their breath, but I look at Mam and begin to giggle. Then I start to laugh. Mam's face is sunken and she remains dead but she's still managed to give me a laugh. People don't know where to look, but I do. I turn to look at them, stare them down. I'm laughing as I shoulder my way through them towards the bathroom. Byrne follows me. Easy now, he says, easy.

I'm laughing as I slam the toilet door and I keep laughing with my head in my hands till I vomit into the shitter. I can hear some commotion outside. A rising chatter, then things go quiet. I wonder if the silence means they're sealing the coffin. I decide to wait. I don't need to see her being locked away forever. No one should see such things.

Never kissed her goodbye.

I turn to wash my face, and catch my reflection before I have time to suck my gut in. I look like a fucking disaster. Funny when that happens, when you see something familiar in a new way. Like you're only really seeing it for the first time –

something you've been blinded to by familiarity. I remember that happening to me once with Mammy. It was a couple of years ago. Some minor arrest. I was in cuffs and being frog-marched through the swinging doors of the station, through the lobby, and there was an old woman standing at the front desk. She was holding a neatly-folded bundle of clothes and giving out reams to a young guard. She turned and looked at me and it took me a second to recognize that it was Mammy. But a second is all it takes; I had caught a glimpse of her from the outside, seen her with the eyes through which the world saw her. And she was old. My Mammy was old. A real old lady. And I wanted to reach out to her in that moment, I don't know why. It was like I wanted to tell her something, do something. Pour some truth of myself through that small chink in the wall of the world. But I didn't reach out, because of the handcuffs.

You okay in there, Byrne says on the other side of the door.

Yeah, I'm fine.

And the funny thing was that the exact same thing happened to Mam; she turned at the sound of the swinging doors and saw me flanked by guards and, for just a second, she didn't recognise me, either. She looked at me with this sort of blank expression. Then her body snapped taut with recognition and her eyes flooded with warmth and she gave me her tired smile, her face like kindness itself, and walked towards me with her arms out by her sides, just like in the coffin, saying she had brought some bits and bobs for me. And I'll always remember that blank expression when she didn't know me. I'll never know what she was seeing.

Colin Walsh was born and raised in Ireland. He has lived in Scotland, France and Quebec and currently lives in Belgium, where he started writing fiction in 2016. 'Seen/Unseen' will be his first published story.

PATRICK HOLLOWAY

Laughing and Turning Away

The first time I had a gun pointed at me I was fourteen and I ran home crying, and my brother laughed at me, calling me *burra*, saying I'd better get used to it. I didn't know if he meant getting used to seeing guns or getting used to being stupid. The second time I was eighteen and I focused on the man's nose, its widening nostrils, how they opened and closed like umbrellas. He told me I had *sorte*, that on another day he would have done much more than just take my phone, wallet, watch, the cross I wore around my neck that grandmother had given me to keep me safe. He would have done much more, he said, because after all, I was *gostosa*, and he slapped my ass and laughed as he walked away.

He walked away. There was no urgency in his step. He wore Havaianas. I did not move. I tried to focus on how his right foot flicked out as it hit the pavement, how his long arms swung by his sides, how his legs, in Rip-Curl shorts, seemed to be hairless. Even now, when I hear the heels of feet slapping against flip-flops I remember his flat nose, how he bit at his bottom lip.

That time I did not run home crying and I did not tell my brother anything, nor my parents, and when they asked where my phone and wallet were I told them I had forgotten to lock the car at university. At lunch on Sunday grandmother noticed the absence of a cross around my neck but said nothing. She frowned slightly at her plate and blessed herself.

So when my father called me telling me I should come home, I should look at flights, that I need to speak to the exchange programme and tell them that it was *urgente,* that maybe I would have to stop my studies for one semester, I was not surprised. There was no sudden intake of breath, or tears running from my eyes, no breathlessness at all. I hung up the phone, sat on my dorm-bed and imagined my brother's face, his pinched little mouth letting words escape. His hands tightening their grip on his phone, on his wallet. And that wide nose and that cocky, favela laugh, and the sound of a thousand people clapping in unison, the very air being twisted around metal.

'Is everything okay?'

My roommate, Sarah – who had once asked me to teach her Spanish, who was amazed that I wore Victoria Secrets and had a Michael Kors bag, and who, open-mouthed shook her head and said, so you guys have Netflix, too? — looked at me with stolen tears. Tears I could not produce. She walked to my bunk and sat next to me and placed her hand on my thigh. Nails the colour of teal. I could not answer her, not in her tongue, instead I thought of the flight path, Wilmington to New York, New York to São Paulo, São Paulo to Porto Alegre. I thought of the hours that awaited me like tops of hills, each hour a hidden land that I could not see.

My brother and I used to go to the street fair on Saturday mornings. The closed-off street stretched all along Redenção park and we'd walk the length of it, picking up old candle sticks to admire before putting them back down, buying fresh pineapple and sweet popcorn. I'd look at the women and how they clung to their men. How when the men tugged a little, they'd follow, without hesitation. I'd watch couples kiss in the park, how one tongue pushed against the other, fighting for space; how teeth just seemed to get in the way. The men's hands always squeezed at something, the chunkiest piece of flesh. I wanted to feel the back of a woman's hand, how it rubbed a cheek downwards, how the fingers pushed through hair and pulled it back slightly.

I had asked my brother, years later, when he was nearly a man and I was experiencing the shame of bleeding for the first time, to never just grab at a woman, to maybe caress her cheek, or play with her hair, and he laughed at me and called me *burra*. It doesn't work like that, he said and laughed a little before turning his back on me and walking away. That is all men seem to do, laugh at women before turning away.

Sarah touched at my cheek, curled my hair behind my ear.

'Talk to me.'

'I feel so *vazia.*'

She curled her fingers in mine and lifted the palm of my hand to her lips.

For seven months I had been teaching her Portuguese, in the quiet of our room, under the warmth of blankets. Her last words before sleep were always, *sonha comigo*. She loved that it was 'dream with me' in Portuguese, she said it was romantic, that it added extra intimacy between the dreamer and the dreamed. For seven months she had guided me around this land that was a distorted reality of the movies. She told me that we don't say hello, how are you, nice to meet you, like I had been taught for as many years as I could remember, but instead, hey, what's up, how's it going. I had met her mother, a doctor, for lunch one day and felt awkward and sweaty when Sarah touched me even though her mother smiled and said we made a lovely couple. She had taught me how to download apps to get discount pizza, and a discount at Abercrombie and Fitch, and a free Uber ride.

I had helped her through the election period. The endless rants, the shouting that entered our room through unseen cracks. Had held her back in a bar when a middle-aged man called her disgusting, a lesbian, Hilary-supporting atrocity. She was not offended by the lesbian comment, she told me later, but by the presumption that she was voting Hilary.

'But you are,' I stated.

'That's not the point.'

When it came to this subject there was little I could do to calm her; there was little I could do in general. I was not, after all, part of the debate, part of their world; just an extra.

I was starving, out of nowhere I wanted my food, feijão and rice and orange slices, and ripe mango peeled and cut into moon shapes, or pinhão, the wooden taste peeled and slipped away, and then something sweet, condensed milk boiled until sticky with chocolate powder. I wanted to eat away my memories. To suck at chimarrão, it's green, dried yerba.

'I'm starving.'

'I'll get us something, stay here, I'll be back in five.'

She took my face in her hands. Her pale blue eyes, like the waters of Fortaleza, studied my face, shivering and flickering. She kissed my forehead and smiled before turning and leaving.

For months I had been thinking about my return back. I had pictured it in December, arriving in that humidity that sits on the tongue like a layer of sand. Had imagined my mother's soft, smiling face rushing towards me at the airport, and my father would wait behind with his emotions somewhere buried in his feet. And we would cook that night, every hob with a pot boiling, and the steam whistling from the pressure cooker with the feijão darkening, and we would drink wine and I would avoid the questions about American men with a remark like, they are too busy pretending to be self-confident to have any confidence at all, and my father would laugh and slap at the table and say, *isso aí*, nothing like a *gaúcho*.

And later, as my brother and father would sit watching TV, I would ask my mother, as we rinsed the dishes, why it was always us to set the table, why we had to wake earlier to make sure breakfast was waiting for them. I would ask her why we close our eyes to their wanderings, why we are the ones who go to the supermarket and iron creases away from a shirt left on the ground; why we bite at our cheeks and swallow our words. And she would look at me, those greying eyes studying the newness in my face, she would maybe smile a little, but she would not answer, that much I knew. And I would want to tell her about Sarah, how she tickled the inside of my arm and sat with me when I woke during the night, *madrugada,* with images of a hundred men smothering me with rough hands. I would want to say, I need you on my side, I can't face them alone. I would go to sleep that night with my arms wrapped around myself and I would cry.

I had been preparing myself for that. Preparing myself for the failure of not telling them about Sarah, preparing to force myself to forget, to delete my Facebook with an excuse that it takes up too much time, to change my email address and erase my photos, one by one, to learn to like the touch of a man.

And now the only man I had ever loved had gone and got himself shot. His utter self-worth as concrete, facing the eye of the gun; I imagine him thinking, I'm Rodrigo Monteiro, I am made for greater things than a bullet. Or he simply would not allow something that was so rightfully his to be taken from him, no matter the value. He was not used to being interrupted at dinner, or called upon from study to answer the front door. He had never been asked to take notes in a meeting because he had the *prettiest* handwriting. Had never been shouted at from a motorbike or whistled at whilst walking the dog. Had never been grabbed at a bar and been turned around violently so a person could get a better look at him. Had never had to defend his choices daily, or smile and bite at his cheeks when a man looked down at him and said it was ambitious to want to study abroad.

Sarah opened the door with a large pizza and a two litre bottle of Coca Cola under her arm. She looked like something from a poster. I imagined a little slogan at her feet. '*Because sometimes it's good not to cook!*' She put them down on the desk and took glasses from a shelf that should store books. The kitchen to the halls was upstairs but we rarely used it. She took a bottle of Bacardi rum from the wardrobe. We were too young to buy alcohol. It wasn't even allowed in the halls, even if you were 21, but my I.D. said 01/12/1987. Which should read, the first of December 1987, but instead read, the 12th of January 1987. So I was illegally legal to buy alcohol. And behind our hanging clothes and piles of shoes were bottles of wine, rum, vodka and tequila.

'Should I go up and get some ice?' She tried to smile but failed.

'No need.'

I could feel the weight of her body on the bed next to mine. Our hips almost touching. The tiniest of space between us, the light green of the sheets could as well have been an ocean. As I took the first bite of the pepperoni pizza I knew that I would vomit. Puke, that was the word I had been told to use. I got up and walked towards the door and she asked if I was okay so I turned, smiled and laughed a little as if to tell her not to worry and went to the communal female bathrooms and puked until I felt weak.

Three days later I was back among my people, my language. I had missed the funeral, which had been the day after his shooting. I had pleaded with my parents to wait but my father dismissed me telling me that it would be crazy, that it would be disrespectful to Rodrigo to leave him sweltering. I cried to my mother. I needed to *see* him. To know that it was really him that had been stolen from the life I had temporarily left behind. I tried not to feel guilty for there was nothing to be guilty about, but at night I still dream that every touch of Sarah brings him one step closer to the bullet.

I had wanted to go back to Wilmington, to run away again, but my father told me my place was, and is, here, with them. Especially at this time. I am finishing university with little interest and I scrub the pots in the evening so hard that sometimes the skin beneath my nails bleed. I never go into Rodrigo's room or answer Sarah's emails. They are both just distant; a step too far away.

Patrick Holloway is an Irish writer who currently teaches and writes in Brazil. His stories and poetry have been published by *Overland, Bath Flash Fiction Anthology* and *Poetry Ireland Review,* among others. His bilingual book of poetry was published in 2016. He's been shortlisted for many awards including The Manchester Fiction Prize and won second prize in The Raymond Carver Short Story Contest, 2017. He would like to dedicate more time to reading and writing but enjoys the better things in life, which require a little bit of money, therefore he divides his time between teaching, writing and travelling. He misses Ireland, a lot. Not so much the weather.

EMILY DEVANE

Then I Am Gone

Fun fairs made Vanessa sad. Perhaps it was the impermanence, the leaving. In autumns past, her sister Ginny had pulled on her arm until she relented, the music booming through their feet, the ground seeming to tremble. 'Okay!' she'd shout, and they'd laugh and stumble their way into a painted car, the safety rail clunking at their laps. Vanessa hated the churning motion, the way their hips knocked from side to side. But she loved the feeling of afterwards, when, drunkenly opening the gate, their hearts would beat at the same gallop. For a few exhilarating minutes, the warm thrill of it lingered.

But the ghostly pale patches of grass, left behind for weeks afterwards, made her forlorn. Other things, too: the bunch of putrefied roses tied to the railings on Bridge Street, the boarded up chippie on the sea front at Queen's Road and now: the coat rack in the hall of 43 Laburnum Crescent, with all its useless, no-longer-worn coats.

Vanessa stood there, brushing her fingers along the empty sleeves. She took Mum's old coat from the hook, the one she and Ginny had laughingly called her 'donkey jacket'. The wool – scarlet, tartan – scratched the delicate skin around the nape of her neck. Not that she cared. She quite liked to feel its scratch.

The thing about having a twin sister who was gone but not officially dead was that it all sounded a bit careless.

I had a sister but I lost her. Somehow she slipped away.

Vanessa couldn't say exactly when it happened. One day, Ginny had simply not come home. She'd left her phone, which was odd. Vanessa checked it sometimes. Ginny's clothes were still in her drawers; her toothpaste was still in the dimple of the basin, the top all crusted over. All she'd taken was a slouchy rucksack and the clothes she wore: the burgundy cardigan that swung awkwardly at her thighs, black leggings, big boots that her bony legs could barely lift. That's how Vanessa had described her to the policeman with the bored face, trying to impress on him some sort of urgency. That was weeks ago.

'Are you off out, love?' Dad called from the lounge. He would be cradling a beer, the first of several.

'Down to the front. Thought I'd take a look, while the fair's still there.' She might have said, *There's a group of us going*, but didn't.

'Well, you take care,' came his voice. Then, with a rustling of paper, the creak of leatherette, the door to the lounge opened just enough for his arm to reach through. 'Here.' He held out a ten-pound-note. 'In case you need it for – whatever.'

Vanessa folded the money away, took a tablet from the almost-empty foil square in her pocket, and dry swallowed. 'It's bound to come in handy. *Whatever* is pretty expensive these days.'

He'd already withdrawn his arm, turned back to the TV. His belly now rose and fell under its ghostly light. *Whatever* was the ultimate in parental abdication. She shut the front door, leaving him to his quiet inebriation, and as she stepped out into the night, her tongue was still bitter with chemicals.

In the photograph over the mantelpiece, she and Ginny

would forever be turning cartwheels on the lawn, daisy chains dangling from their necks, hair in plaits the colour of corn, tapering to thin wisps half-way down their arms. Unadorned, then, by pieces of metal. Her hair undyed, her skin unmarked.

Everyone has their own way, Dad had said.

The fairground was coming to an end. Some of the rides were already gone. A narrow strip on the car park along the harbour wall remained. Soon, the trucks would leave, piled high with pieces of helter skelter and gaudy lights and rigging. Off to some other seaside town for bonfire night. Perhaps Ginny had hitched a lift on some godawful truck, wedged in among the waltzers. Anything to disappear.

In the candy floss queue was a dark-clothed girl. Ginny had that same way of hanging her neck, of twisting her feet around each other at the ankles, of folding her arms, as if making a knot of herself. But Vanessa didn't want candy floss. Ginny wouldn't let it pass her lips. She looked again. The way the girl laughed, with her head tilted back, was all wrong.

Vanessa walked on past the stalls: soft toys strung up above a pool of bobbing ducks, coconut shy – the usual thing. Near the sea wall, a caravan proclaimed: *Madame Zelda Knows Your Future*. Something woollen was strung on a plastic chair – it could even be burgundy. Vanessa thought about poking her head through the door, taking a look at this Madame Zelda, just in case she had more of an inkling than the bored-faced policeman. Vanessa stood outside long enough to take in the crystal ball, a wisp of incense smoke threading across it. A middle-aged woman in a polyester tunic was reading a magazine.

'Can I help you?' Zelda said, without enthusiasm.

Vanessa shook her head, no. 'Just looking for someone. I thought this might be hers.' Vanessa touched the burgundy wool. It was damp.

Zelda looked at her with inscrutable eyes. If she knew something about Vanessa's future, she wasn't saying.

Next door stood a wooden caravan, the old-fashioned type. A man perched on the bottom step with a handful of flyers, not so very different to the missing person posters she'd been urging into people's hands for weeks now. Back when Dad had still gone in to work, he'd printed off a job lot on the photocopier. He'd done something to the dimensions; distorted the photograph, leaving Ginny a thin smear of black on the page.

Business was evidently slow at *Freak Show: A Nostalgic Journey Through Time*.

'Fancy a look inside? Be freaked out or your money back,' the man said. His face drooped slightly to one side.

'Go on, then,' Vanessa said.

Inside, the caravan was lit by lamps with green bulbs, giving it an Oz-like glow. She rubbed her head. The tablets were on prescription from Dr. Wilding. He said they might help with the feelings. But they had been making her brain hurt, re-ordering things inside her head so that sounds appeared wonky, as if refracted and churned out upside down. Glass cabinets along the caravan's inner edges contained jars of what she assumed to be body parts suspended in chemicals. *Frederick III of Denmark was a collector of pickled punks*, said one label. Vanessa recoiled at the shrimp-like creature within. A large glass box contained a stuffed lamb with two glassy-eyed heads. Photographs of giants and dwarves lined the walls. *Lobster Boy*, *The Lion-Faced Man*, *Camel Girl*, *The Man with the Rubber Skin*.

She imagined one for Ginny: *Moon Girl, quite literally disappears in front of your very eyes*. Her twin had been getting smaller for a while; smaller and paler, her edges fuzzier. By the time she had gone, there was very little left of her.

One photograph showed two men in an awkward embrace. The man on the right seemed to be wrestling to get away from the other. Something about their proximity was fascinating. Vanessa drew closer to observe the men's locked grimaces and saw that they were, in fact, joined at the chest. Pinned beside the picture was a yellowing newspaper article. These two had toured the world, fathered more than twenty children between them, had even owned slaves. One had been a drinker, while the other had abstained. Their death cast was in some museum.

'Fascinating story, isn't it?'

Vanessa cried out, then gasped at the sight of the man with the drooping face, who now stood beside her.

'Do you know much about them?' she said.

'Only as much as anyone else. They were clever. Taken from Thailand as boys. People say they could play chess. This one,' – he pointed at the larger twin – 'had a head for poker. His brother liked a drink.'

'They never had surgery?'

'No doctor could do it. The other one, the drinker, died first. Imagine that? Waking up to find your brother, dead beside you.'

For Vanessa, it wasn't hard to imagine.

'Poor man died of shock before they could separate them. Even if they had, he wouldn't have survived.

Vanessa pointed at the smaller twin. 'So, this one was the first to go?'

'That's right. Looked like he was trying to get away all along, I always thought.'

Vanessa looked again at the photograph, the men's closeness. She saw in their faces strangled, put-upon smiles.

The man took a roll-up out of his pocket. 'You interested in these things?'

'I guess. How people seem to others, how they seem to themselves.' Vanessa reached into her bag. 'I'm looking for someone, actually. Thought she might be here. Can I give you one of these, just in case?' She unfurled a flyer.

'I see,' said the man, looking at Ginny's stretched smear of a face. 'Looks a bit like you. If I see her I'll…'

'You won't.' said Vanessa. 'See her, I mean. It just makes me feel better.'

He nodded. 'Dead tonight. Time to go.' The good side of his face was almost handsome, she thought. Not quite handsome – but almost. He cupped one hand around the other and lit the roll-up.

'And how do you find that?'

'The going, you mean?'

'Must be hard, never staying put.'

'Not for me. I don't think I could stand to stay.' He breathed out a plume of smoke. '*Then I am gone*. Those were his final words, you know.' He pointed at the pair on the wall, locked forever in that awkward embrace.

Because of the wind, the big wheel was closed. Vanessa headed to the waltzers. If Ginny was here, that's where she'd be. Ginny liked music that made her veins pulse. Ginny liked clothes that drowned her. *Scream if you want to go faster!* said the sign, but Vanessa was too busy clutching the metal bar. The mirrored panes in the centre flashed scarlet each time she passed: scarlet and burgundy, burgundy and scarlet.

When Ginny got her first tattoo, Vanessa had thought it was a joke, one of those transfers. The pocket watch, swirled with leaves and branches, was forever stopped on a quarter to twelve. Ginny's arms were soon covered, as if creeping ivy had slowly covered the freckled skin beneath. And as her arms thinned, the pictures shrank too. *Why are you not more bothered about this?* She wanted to ask Dad but she knew what he'd say. *People have their own way*, he'd say, like he'd said about Mum and everything since.

As Vanessa's car turned, she saw a girl. The girl stood beside the ride, the exact same size as Ginny. But the hair was wrong and the face, too round. Too healthy. Vanessa knew it wasn't her. She saw her sister everywhere: that slouchy cardigan, the ink black hair, the frail wrists. This time, though, the girl was staring. Really staring.

Vanessa stared back. The girl's mouth broke into a dimpled smile.

Sounds warped and bent in time with the pulsing behind her ears. The wind whipped at her bare neck. As the metal bar lifted, she wrapped Mum's coat more tightly around herself and searched the crowd. She thought she saw her – the girl – skirting the side of the carousel, weaving her way past a painted wooden gondola, heading towards the *Maze of Mirrors*.

Mum wasn't dead. She'd left on the 11.45, had even written it in the calendar along with a reminder about the dentist's. There had never been an apology, just a *People have their own way* from Dad and the expectation that everything would be okay, wouldn't it? Except her girls hadn't taken it so well. The time was etched into Ginny's skin. And the more Vanessa had clung to her, the more her sister had pulled away.

The mirror maze was like the centre of an explosion. Each splintered piece of glass set at an angle, designed to confuse. The mirrors moved the light so that when Vanessa held out her hand, she forgot which hand she held up, or which image was true. In one, she swelled as if helium-filled; in another, she narrowed to the thinnest of crescents. Far away, she thought she saw the swing of a girl's cardigan but then, it was gone. She'd quite lost sight of the door from which she had come and the chemical buzz was fading into something else, something far more real: the hollowed out feeling of pain and grief. And she knew that she was on the brink of disappearing, too, as if she'd woken to find herself attached to a body that had died. *Stop the clocks!* Ginny, had said. Ginny, who'd tried to shrink herself small, back to a time before they were motherless.

'Then I am gone,' Vanessa said to the thin-faced girl in the mirror. She was surprised at the smile on the girl's lips. The lips were moving while hers were still. She held her fingers to the glass and pressed gently.

Emily Devane lives and writes in Yorkshire. Her short stories have been published in *The Lonely Crowd* and *The Nottingham Review*, among others. She has won prizes for her flash fiction, including The Bath Flash Fiction Award (February 2017) for her story 'The Hand That Wields The Priest'. In 2016, Emily was selected for the Word Factory apprenticeship scheme. She recently received a Northern Writers' Award for her short story collection in progress. She is also working on a novel based on a character from one of her short stories and tweets at @DevaneEmily.

CATHERINE FINCH

Paid in Full

I found him in the river; leather boots, trouser legs, soldier's jacket. His face rippled under the quiet water, the features separating and reforming. Curiosity gripped and I stared.

I recall pushing him with my toe, watching the body move like the logs and branches that float downstream after heavy rain and catch between rocks. I glanced round, then slid two fingers in his pocket teasing out a whistle and a penknife and a photograph of a lady with dark hair. Finally, before panic, and the urge to escape overtook me, I released a few small coins.

A boy of strange and curious ways, I was a collector; pebbles, rusty shards of metal, coloured glass pieces, animal bones. I risked friendship to steal ribbons or pencils from the other children. I risked punishment if my aunt found my treasures, so I hid them. A loose floorboard in the barn could be prised up, or a brick removed from a wall. Discovery haunted me; harsh fingers handling precious things, stealing my collections. In the end, a careless hiding place twisted the course of my life, destroyed the lives of others, loaded my soul with a bitter, impossible debt.

Today, my head is full of disturbing thoughts and the afternoon heat oppresses. I refuse my cane, but I am grateful for Fabienne's arm and the tall figure of my grandson close by. She is a sweet girl and I see the love she has for Stefan.

'Do you feel up to a short walk?' she asks. 'Surely you want to see the village now we're here. We can return to the car if you get too hot.'

She tells Stefan to get my hat, and it is placed gently on my head.

We walk and I notice the cart, abandoned long ago, as if the horse was released for the last time and the carrier let the shafts fall to the ground. As we pass, I pause to touch the letters of his name, faint colours across the rough planks. I remember myself as a child of three who sat in this cart and howled all the way from the station. I stopped when my aunt gave me an unexpected cuff and shouted, 'Shut up, that's enough.'

Should I go into the village? So much time has passed. Yet someone may recognise the turn of my head, a strand of hair, a look that unsettles a memory. I grip Fabienne's arm and we walk towards the Maison de Maitre. She remarks how pretty it is. Stefan fiddles with his expensive camera. He is a collector of photographs, a safe, two dimensional pastime. Later, he will tinker with the images on a screen, enhancing colours, smoothing imperfections, polishing the captured memory.

We pose in front of the gates.

'Do you remember this house, Papi?' Fabienne asks, and I reply that I do. She sees the geraniums tumbling over the balustrade which frames the double staircase up to the door. Years ago, my aunt had grumbled at this extravagance.

'They need two staircases?' she protested to Uncle Jean. 'Madame doesn't have to sweep them herself, that's for sure.'

I look up to the flowers, the twisted ironwork, the crafted stone, and I see soldiers, Monsieur Delpech in pyjamas, his face red, his eyes full of fear. I see a woman crying, children clutching at her dress. The sound fills my ears. Fabienne's chatter, whilst not unpleasant, seems distant.

It is a cloudless sky and I am glad of my hat. I wear long trousers and sleeves now, after all, who wants to look at the thin arms and shapeless skin of an old person? Yet as a child, I put on the same rags every day, garments fashioned from curtains, old clothes, even the sacks that held the grain. My aunt was as resourceful as the rest during the occupation, but only when her own children had been clothed, did she look to me.

The little bar tabac is still here, and I recall the dark interior, thick with cigarette smoke. If Madame Celeste had sweets, we huddled around the counter with our coins and were usually rewarded with a morsel of something pink or red which brought a brief shot of sugar to sweeten our lives. Our fathers and uncles sat with glasses of pastis, the alcohol softening their faces, gentling their hands. On the farm it was a cuff or a slap. In the bar they ruffled heads and patted shoulders. The figure of poor Jean-Marc is still clear, a noisy, ebullient drinker, dragged home by his wife most evenings. We would watch, then mimic his drunken capers, each of us exaggerating the loose limbs and slurred voice.

If the soldiers came in, the men drank up and left, coins placed quietly on the counter.

The bar is closed, so we walk on towards the Mairie and the church.

'How pretty,' Fabienne exclaims. 'What beautiful stonework.'

I hear the click of the camera behind me. City youngsters. They see the charm of this village. I gaze at the steps leading to the church door and I see desperation, injustice, and I feel the burden of shame I shouldered as a boy and have carried for a lifetime.

We sit outside the Mairie and they leave me to rest as they visit the church. He takes her hand. She reaches up and kisses him with a smile full of promise. I am jealous of their youth yet grateful they can enjoy it. At their age I was already old.

A crowd of us would meet at the river, but the day I saw him I was fishing alone. I wanted to run, but found no movement in my legs. Then, the urge to search his wet pockets, to take possession of whatever I found, took hold. With dripping fingers, I stowed the items in my bag and glanced over his face. It was pale, like the flesh of a dead fish, stripped of its silver scales. Turning away in disgust, I fell over a rock in the shallow water and splashed wildly for a moment, trying to regain my balance. Calm tipped into panic and I reached the bank with frantic ungainly strides. The firmer ground gave my legs momentum and they sprinted me back to the village, my stolen goods rattling.

My mind was already working on a hiding place. It would be too dark to make things out in the barn, so I chose a loose stone in the wall opposite the post office. The stone came out easily. I hesitated before replacing it, chose one coin to keep, taking a moment to turn its foreignness over in my fingers. I walked home through the village, catching my breath.

'Where've you been?' My aunt was waiting. 'Disappearing again, when you have jobs to do. Get on with them before it's too dark.'

Dodging her raised hand, I touched the surface of the coin in my pocket and felt glad.

'Papi.' A voice weaves through the memories and I feel a gentle touch on my arm. I turn my head and see Stefan's face.

'You're tired,' he says. 'Shall we go back?'

I think about this.

'We can go past the post office,' I say. 'It isn't much further.'

Fabienne eases me to my feet and we make our way through the houses. The road is dusty, hot. Shutters are closed and there is no one to notice us. She tries to lead me to the pavement, but I resist and we continue across the road to the hiding place. It isn't there. I needn't search for it as the wall has been rebuilt.

There is one stone, slightly larger than the others, with a metal plate, a little tarnished, but the lettering is clear. Fingering the small coin in the pocket of my trousers, I reach out and touch the names: Arnaud Delpech, Celeste Balat, Jean-Marc Fournier. Mort pour la France.

'Did you know these people?' Fabienne asks, and I nod, but offer no explanation.

'How sad,' she says, and the three of us stand in quiet thought and I remember.

Soldiers marched in, tearing apart a soft grey dawn, shouting orders in harsh, twisted French, clattering on doors. We were herded into the square, some still in night clothes, others rough-haired and unwashed. I was sent to get my cousin who was at the pump and I saw them forcing the mayor from his home.

Men held their wives, women grasped their children. In the faces around me I saw defiance, hatred, fear, and I twisted my fingers to stop them shaking. Officers stood on the steps to the church. A whistle, a penknife and a handful of coins lay on the floor; my treasures, discovered. I tried to speak, but children were pushed to the back where the school teacher encircled us with his arms whispering words of calm. We heard accusing voices, then shouts, then cries.

Finally, three shots.

As the marching feet receded, a subdued wailing began, rising up until words of fury punctured the sorrow. Children found their parents, but I crept away and hid in the barn.

When my aunt and uncle returned they dragged me from my hiding place. She pinched my arm and pressed her wet, angry face close to mine.

'What do you know?' she hissed. 'Madame Delacroix saw you hiding something in the wall. And what's this?' She held out the German coin. 'I found it in your pocket.'

She let my cheek take the full force of her outstretched hand and shouted, 'Tell me.'

'The body, it was in the river, it was already dead.' I faltered over the words. 'I - I just took some things and hid them.'

The fury was uncontrollable, her hand, a fist, her mouth venomous and foul. In the end my uncle dragged her away. The last words I remember were, 'My friends, they are murdered because of you.'

I touched the hurt places, watched tears drip through my fingers to the dust and felt each sob like a rough shock. Darkness fell and I was afraid to be alone. I wiped my nose and face on my sleeve and reached up to try the door. It was jammed from the other side. I pleaded, rattled the wood, but each time I stopped and listened, I heard only the stirring of the animals and the frantic clicking of the cicadas. My bare foot touched something under the straw. Reaching down, my fingers closed around the coin. I lay on the straw like an animal and slept.

The next day, Uncle took me to the station and put me on the train to Paris, back to my father.

I feel the softness of Fabienne's hand. She lifts the brim of my hat to look into my face.

'Why did you want to come back?' she asks. 'I think you have a story about this village that you haven't told us.'

I push my hat from my forehead, try to recall why I decided to return after so many years, and, in the muddle of my thoughts, there is one clear thread, and I know.

'I have a debt to repay,' I offer.

'From so long ago? You were only a boy.'

I am silent. My thinking, like my limbs, is slow. It needs time to separate each thought and drop it into place.

'Papi, you are the kindest man. You have spent your life helping others.' She looks again into my face and I briefly lift my eyes to meet hers. 'Whatever happened when you lived here, you have paid your debt.'

I consider her words. I think about the three who paid for

me. In my life I have tried to pay, so many times, in so many ways, but I have discovered that release from the magnitude of my wrong comes at an impossible price. The Bank of Atonement is, indeed, a foreboding place. No withdrawals at this establishment, only deposits against huge, life-sapping debt.

'We love you Papi,' Fabienne says, and I meet her eyes with a slow gratitude. She takes my hand between her hands, but does not ask for more.

So many years ago. I was such a little scrap of life.

As we pass the cart on our way back to the car, I feel in my pocket and draw out the small German coin, worthless now, priceless as the means to finally settle my account. I have carried it for far too long. It is time to let go. I look briefly in the palm of my hand, then I push the coin into the soil beneath the flowers, burying it deep. I experience a lightness of spirit, a weight lifted, a final reckoning settled.

I glance towards the young people striding out in front hands touching, their lives, their memories, pure. Hope is in the next generation. It envelops me, opening my eyes to truth, bringing a glimpse of peace, finally.

And my debt to this village, to Monsieur Delpech, Madame Celeste and Jean-Marc; paid in full.

During her 30 years in teaching, **Catherine Finch** wrote lovely stories, plays and musicals for children and tedious documents for school inspectors. Although reluctant to leave the village school where she was head teacher, she is delighted to have found space in her life for some real writing. She has been shortlisted and placed in a number of competitions, including Flash 500 and TSS, and has completed two novels.

Catherine is married and has two grown-up children. She divides her time between Lancashire and South West France, and is indebted to the Parisot Writing Group for their enthusiasm and encouragement.

https://twitter.com/chatffinch

BRIDGITTE CUMMINGS

Hollow

They never told us about the freezing mists, the grease of freshly boiled flesh, the endless slosh and slide of disinfectant across the long line of shiny steel benches. Instead, they told us it was £6 an hour. 6am start. Minibus stopping at the old racetrack bridge. No waiting. You miss the bus, you miss your shift, you miss a day and a half's pay. Not legal, but what can you do when half of them working here are illegals.

'Welcome back.' Limpdick nudges me from behind, knocking my hip sharply into the edge of the bench as he breathes last night's curry into my ear. My knife skids across the wet chicken carcass and air-kisses my knuckles. I tighten my throat, strangle down a curse. The blade is as dull and blunted as my line manager's intellect, but I still hold on to the fantasy of plunging it cleanly into his heart. 'Stop staring into space, Princess. No more chances.'

He calls me Princess because I wear a bit of make-up. I even wear deodorant. Imagine that. Such airs. Not that Limpdick would know about deodorant. He makes a rat's arse smell sweet.

'Speed up or fuck off back to your palace.' The twisted grin threatens to trigger an eruption of pustules stretched across his cheeks. He stands close and reaches out to the naked chicken, which is attempting a swift retreat down the assembly belt. It clings to its stand, preferring blunt-knife butchery to the grubby nicotine-stained pawing of Limpdick. I know what's coming. Limpdick yanks off the carcass, flicks it onto its back, examines the cut of the wing, and then shakes his head at me. 'Untidy.' He rams the bird back onto its cone, sending an arc of cool fleshy droplets into the air. He smirks. 'No, one likes a scraggy bird, Kassie.'

'Processing,' they had called it. The advert lurked at the back of the free newspaper, a smudgy insert between the jaunty offers for speedy loans and discrete massage. The moment I showed Angie the job advert I knew we would apply. She squinted, her tongue tunnelling furiously into her cheek as she absorbed each word. Then her ball-bearing eyes rolled up beneath the curly red fringe and shone.

'Fucking cool,' she whooped. 'Told you something would come up.'

I forced a smile. Job offers for two unskilled eighteen year olds had been in short supply, even before the closure of the hospital. It was a job, sure, but hardly a highflying career opportunity. Then again, what did I expect? I'd thrown away my chances over four months ago, on that cool, speckled night when the rain began to spit. The ticket shelter at the back of the railway car park had reeked of stale urine, but at least it had been dry. He'd been nice, that guy, not like some of the others we met down at the club, but I knew as swiftly as he fastened up his trousers, that I would not see him again.

Angie nudges away a short Filipino girl and slots herself neatly beside me. 'So, where were you last week?'

I look over my shoulder. Limpdick is further up, cracking on to some blonde newbie who still feels obliged to give a polite smile in response to his exploratory hands.

'I tried calling a dozen times,' she says, reaching over and slicing through the squat parcels of flesh like a Samurai on speed. 'I was worried.'

'I lost it.'

Angie's knife hovers motionless in the air. 'What?'

'I lost the baby.'

'Oh Kas, I'm sorry, hun.' She stares at me as I resume hacking into the chickens. 'You okay?'

'Yeah. I'm fine now. Miscarriage. Happens a lot, apparently.'

'Wanna come stay with me for a bit?'

I shake my head too vigorously, as if I could send my tears out into the cold misty spray of the factory. But they are iron heavy, anchored somewhere deep and dark inside of me. I pass the knife into my left hand, uncurling and waggling the stiffening fingers on my right. They are already getting numb, heavy and clumsy, as if thickly coated in wax. A cluster of slick blisters in my palm begins to pulse beneath the latex glove, and I feel a combination of relief and pain as I stretch my fingers back against the bench.

Angie does not let up speed. Her hands are smaller than mine, but they move with a fluidity my fingers can never hope to possess. Her knife is a conductor's baton, slicing through the wet carcasses, whilst her gaze sweeps across the factory floor and her ears tune into commentary inaudible to me above the clashing orchestra of production. She doesn't understand my restless jousting with the clock. She possesses a resilience I admire and envy. Angie can escape with her thoughts any time she chooses, whilst mine remain shackled here to the bench, imprisoned in this cold, deafening chamber for ten hours a day.

'How 'bout coming to The George, later?' Angie says.

'Nah, not tonight.'

'They got a band and curry night on,' she urges. 'Go on, Kas. I fancy an Indian.'

'Thought your Gary was Italian,' I reply, with only a twitch of my lips.

Angie casts a swift look behind, then slaps a chicken against the side of my head, dislodging the giant cobweb of a hairnet. 'Alright, Miss Clever-Gobb.'

I grin, hastily scooping back my hair.

'Isn't it about time you used that brain for something other than sarcasm?' She stares at me, her face suddenly serious.

I laugh, and cringe inwardly on hearing how forced it sounds. I've been butchering chickens for almost three months now. Could have re-taken my exams, been out there looking for a proper job, maybe even started college.

A horn blasts three times from the other side of the shed, and the chickens wobble on their cones as the belt growls to a halt.

'Gutting machine on the blink again,' mutters Angie.

Limpdick shuffles over to the head of the assembly line.

'Okay, need ten of you down at Op One Evisceration.' No longer competing with the clang of the conveyer belt, Limpdick's voice ricochets sharply across the steel walls of the shed. He scans the line, one arm rising up from the folds of his oversized overall. I try to step back, but the cold metallic edge of the table jabs into my spine like the butt of a rifle.

'Not gut yanking,' spits Angie. 'That makes me fucking heave.'

'I'm not doing it,' I say, but my voice is too quiet for her to hear, and I can already see Limpdick heading down the line, pointing at girls who are slow or have fallen out of favour.

I suddenly feel sick, and I know I can't do it. Once before I did it, wrenching out grey, eely intestines from still-warm flesh and feeling them slither and slide under my plastic glove. The smell in the section was nauseating, a thick stench clinging onto my nostril hairs like rancid dew, but it was the act that made me retch – hollowing them out.

Six girls peel away from the line, singled out, throwing scowls at Limpdick's back.

'Get going, Princess.' Limpdick jerks his thumb at me. It

is not until he has almost moved past me that he notices the shake of my head. 'Now.'

I pull my shoulders back and brace my legs for support. They feel stronger than I expect. Not weak and trembling like last week, when I had made the call, and prayed silently they would give me a pill, knowing deep down they wouldn't, even before they had examined me with prodding fingers and sympathetic smiles. I had left it too late. Hoped it would go away. Thought I could keep it hidden, like the morning sickness which had messed up my exams, like the overwhelming tiredness which had consumed me after every shift, like the fear I might be imprisoned here with people like Limpdick, for the rest of my life.

There is a momentary flicker of uncertainty in Limpdick's face before anger replaces it. His lips tighten. I shuffle back as he moves closer, and feel the smooth shaft of the knife beneath my fingers.

'Last chance, Princess.'

I stand rigid, not looking at him, but over him. I think of last week, in that room: the stench of disinfectant, the gleaming metallic surfaces, latex gloves, cold light searing through my tightly closed lids. Part of me had been hollowed out that morning.

Angie steps towards me but I shake my head. I need to do this on my own. The knife clatters behind me as I let go of it and the bench. I stride past Limpdick and catch a small smile of satisfaction twitching his features. But I do not join the other girls leaning against the wall. Instead, I walk past them.

I pull at the hefty double doors and slip through. I carry my hollowness with me, perhaps always will, but in this moment as I leave behind the mists, and smell, and noise, the weight seems just a little less heavy to bear.

Bridgitte Cummings was born in the UK but is now resident in Australia. She has had short stories published in both the UK and Australia, including publication in the Australian *Big Issue Fiction Edition 2016*. She is currently working on her first novel.

ALEXANDER KNIGHTS

Nico and Molière

Nico is sitting at the champagne bar in St Pancras Station, waiting for Molière. Not the playwright. He's dead. Nico's never seen or read a Molière play – it's just what he calls his girlfriend, Molly. Molly calls him Nico. Everyone else calls him Nick, but Nico sounds more French, and that's what they're going to be – well, Parisians anyway – instead of boring old Londoners.

It's 7.20am by the great gilt-edged disc that hangs over the Eurostar platforms and the station terrace. Nico's never drunk champagne this early. Never drunk any booze this early. But this is the moment when Nico and Molière took their lives in hand, when they took a different fork. Shame Molière's late.

Technically, it's still summer, but Nico wouldn't mind a scarf. It's freezing up here on the terrace. All the trains ready to leave behind the glass partition. Molière will be wearing a scarf, a small silk one, maybe that blue-and-white one with the arabesque patterns. *Classique. Exotique.* That's her style. As is being late.

They should've travelled here together. They should've both stayed at her dad's. But he also had to say *au revoir* to his parents. Oh Nicholas, are you sure this is a good idea?

Another sip of champagne. A pound a sip, if he takes one large enough to feel the bubbles burn. Maybe he'll buy himself another glass when Molière gets here. They can down them together before they scoot to the departure lounge. The 8.31 to the Gare du Nord. It was always Molly's dream – now it's his too.

Why the hell is she cooking her Dad breakfast? This early. And with so little time. A full English! Hardly appropriate in his condition. A walking heart attack. Never mind... as long as she gets here by 7.45, they can quaff their drinks and they'll still have enough time.

Always a bit late. Lovable, usually. Like that first time when she burst into the screen-printing class – hair at sixes and sevens, but still somehow artful above that honey-coloured trench coat and the tote bag with raindrops. She smiled so sweetly as the teacher went through the basics again, and Nico was dying to know what had held up this latecomer.

It took a while to get talking. She worked on her stencil design with a quiet intensity, while he dithered over some photos he'd brought – all too fussy, too detailed, to make a bold and simple print. By the time he'd settled on the close-up of a clock-face, Molière was almost ready to prepare her silkscreen. Her design was empty chairs. A bunch of them in a park.

'Le Jardin du Luxembourg,' she said, catching him looking. 'The chairs are very distinctive.'

'Oh yeah,' he said, with a *soupçon* of recognition. 'Well, yours is going to look better than mine.'

'They're so elegant and mysterious,' she said – always one to deflect a compliment, always with the quiver of a smile. 'I'd like to capture a little of that mystery.'

'You go there often? To Paris?'

'Hardly ever. Dad never liked to when I was young. A

French girl broke his heart. He used to live in Montparnasse. Saw Samuel Beckett in a bar. Had his favourite bakery. Took amazing black-and-white shots with his Leica, like this one.' She flattened out the picture she'd been tracing. Empty chairs in the Jardin du Luxembourg.

'Oh wow, he took this?'

'Paris in the 80s,' she said, dreamily. 'The ripped jeans, the shoulder pads – oh man! But a lot of Dad's street scenes are timeless, you know? I'm going to live there one day. In Paris. What's the point of speaking French if you're not going to live there? I'm certainly not going to be a French teacher all my life, that's for sure.'

Nico raises his champagne glass in a silent toast. Somebody below on the station concourse is playing one of those plinky public pianos. The tune from '2001: A Space Odyssey' when the ship docks at the space station. *Dah dah dah dah dah, ting ting, ting ting. Dah dah dah dah dah, ting ting, ting ting.* A text flashes on his phone.

> Molly, 7.24am: 'Baby! The Central Line is down! Just our luck. Walking to Shep's Bush Market to get the Circle. Be there at 8am. Don't panic!'
>
> Molly, 7.25am: 'Sorry baby xxx'
>
> Molly, 7.26am: 'You said half an hour's fine for check in, right?'

Yes, for an emergency! Not a farewell breakfast for your Dad. You already cooked him beef bourguignon last night. And made *îles flottantes*. That's what we had for our first dinner at your place. Meringues like mountains. *Crème anglaise*.

Nico stares at the leather banquette. It's the colour of the tiles on the walls of old Underground stations. Ox-blood red. Molière would love it.

This little habit of lateness. Always a few minutes here and there, the near misses, the theatre doors closing, tiptoeing into darkened rooms, whispered apologies, his mother turning in the pew at his cousin's wedding. Oh Nicholas, late again – that's your party trick, isn't it?

It's like when he'd leave his dinner unfinished as a kid – used to drive his mother crackers. Not quite committed to the task in hand. Holding something back. But then he grew up. Not my party trick. Not mine.

Psssssssh! A train releases its brakes.

They won't know anyone in Paris. They'll be alone together.

Nick, 7.27am: 'Don't worry, my love. See you by the entrance!'

Oh Paris! That autumn half-term a couple of years ago. Just visiting. No thoughts of quitting their jobs, ending their lease, boxing up their stuff. It was all about London then. Before Molière became acting head of the languages department. Before it all became *un peu trop.* He knew it would be – as soon as she took the promotion. But if not that, then not this, so a year of hell had been worth it. 'Hell is other people,' wrote Sartre. Other people's parents, thinks Nico. Her pupils' parents. Her dad...

She was always talking about that trip. Nico and Molière in Paris. Their midnight walk along the deserted arcades of the Palais Royal, the funny way the doors whine on the Metro before they wheeze shut, that sunny morning in the Place des Vosges and the wet cobbles in Montmartre. They'd loved that corner café with the mirrored walls, but what about those bones in the Catacombs?

Fwoch, fwoch, fwoch! An espresso machine froths in the distance. Nico's champagne is going flat.

Of course, before Nico and Molière there was Nick and Molly. And he could've talked just as much about their happy summer evenings on the National Theatre terrace and their misty winter strolls in the parks, how they found the low drone of planes quite sad, but were cheered by houseboat chimney smoke, pollarded trees with their knuckles in the air, all the sash windows…

Molly, 7.41am: 'At Shep's BM – train in 2!'

Nico's always been the practical one. Just gave her sensible reasons for their life in London. Nothing poetic. Friends, family, work. They knew what they were doing in London. They knew how to get along. But the way she talked about Paris…

He drains his champagne and lugs his bags to the escalator.

Nick, 7.46am: 'I'll be by the entrance. Call me as soon as you get to St P.'

Empty chairs. *Îles flottantes.* It was just a dream for her. But he made it real. Even proposed it in that year of hell – convinced her. They'd get a studio flat in the Bastille. She'd do a screen-printing MA. He'd teach in a school – English as a Foreign Language.

Nico and Molière. Let's live in Paris!

Molly, 8.14am: missed calls (4).

Molly, 8.16am: 'I'm at the entrance. Where are you?'

Nick, 8.22am: 'I'm on the train.'

Molly, 8.22am: 'But you have the tickets.'

Molly, 8.24am: missed calls (2).

Nick, 8.26am: 'You don't want this. You love London.'

Nick, 8.27am: 'And there's your dad.'

Molly, 8.27am: 'Answer your phone!'

Molly, 8.28am: 'Nico!!'

Nick, 8.31am: 'I'm sorry, Molière. Merci pour tout.'

He wants to text 'I love you', but the train has left the station.

Alexander Knights spent ten years as a travel guide editor and loves writing stories inspired by places. His London tales come out of a fascination with the city he has lived in for most of his adult life and he also blogs about this great labyrinth at www.londonimagined.com He has an MA in creative writing from Birkbeck and has published short stories in *Litro Magazine, Riptide Journal* and *The Mechanics' Institute Review.*

MARA BLAZIC

Bionic Girl

On days like this eight-year-old Boyanna wishes she had a
bionic ear.

She claps and bounces in her pink flip-flops across the
scorching hopscotch court in the empty schoolyard. HOP!
JUMP! HOP! HOP!

As she spins around to leap back down the squares, she sees
him. He's on that rusty black dirt bike, tearing towards her.

Her little feet freeze.

Her heart sinks.

Her face falls.

Bionic hearing would've picked up his approach.

There's no time to run for the tipi as Ned skids within a
centimeter of her toes. He lands his shabby sneakers on the
parched bitumen, leans on his handle bars, 'Watchya doin' Boy?
Wanna play?' Despite the searing January heat he's dressed top
to toe in black. Today he's also got a black eye.

'Play what?' Whenever he appears he turns the playground
into an outdoor torture chamber.

'Pley vot?' he parrots her accent.

Ned is ten. His English is better than hers, his parents have been in Australia longer. They live three doors down on Botting Street. Despite being from different parts of Yugoslavia, their mums are friends and catch the train together in their denim overalls to work at the Holden car factory. Their dads lay bricks and share beers on building sites.

She's not sure about Ned's dad, but hers comes home drunk, words get nasty and loud and full plates of pork and vegetables shatter against the kitchen's lime green walls.

This is when Boyanna flees to her room she shares with her dolls and Max her golden teddy bear. She'd like him to be bigger as he's named after Jaime Sommer's bionic German Shepherd, who's scared of fire. Boyanna makes sure her Max is never near the kerosene heater during winter. There's a small color pin-up poster of Jaime above her bed from an old TV Guide magazine her neighbor chucked away. It says 'Lindsay Wagner The Bionic Woman'. She's in that blue, white and red tracksuit Boyanna would love to have. On the tiny TV in the sitting room Jaime's clothes are always grey.

She dreams of the real Bionic Woman doll (it has all her bionic parts!), but this Serbian Christmas came and went on January 7 and Deda Mraz didn't bring her one. She wonders if it's because they don't have a chimney. More than anything she wishes she too had bionic legs, taking her far, far away from Botting Street.

'Run Boyanna Run!!' she screams to herself as Ned's sneakers land back on his pedals. She can feel his bike's thick tyre against her flip-flops.

He hunts her around the splintered wooden seesaw, the one he leapt from causing her to abruptly drop and badly bruise her bum. She couldn't walk properly for a week. That day too he demanded she play with him, 'Let's seesaw Boy!'

Having no money for babysitters, Boyanna's parents lock

her inside alone during the school holidays. The house becomes so hot she has to escape. From the slippery bathtub she mounts the wobbly hand basin, climbs through the bathroom window and pretends her bionic legs – *tch-tch-tch-tch* – are touching down in her mum's cucumber patch – *tch-tch-tch-tch* – and sprinting through the backyard – *tch-tch-tch-tch* – along the driveway – *tch-tch-tch-tch* – and across Botting Street – *tch-tch-tch-tch* – straight into the empty school playground.

She can't seem to shake Ned as she runs around the roundabout. Once he spun the disk really fast, then just pushed her off. She smashed her chin, chipped her front tooth on the bitumen. She looks horrible in last year's class of '77 photo.

Trying to reach higher ground she sprints for the monkey bars, but Ned's too fast and his dirt bike plows into her.

CRASH!

Her body flips forward.

She closes her terrified eyes.

She spreads her little palms out towards the blazing concrete to cushion the fall.

Her body freezes in mid-air. She hears the familiar electronic bionic sound – *tch-tch-tch-tch* – and in slow motion she rights herself – *tch-tch-tch-tch* – and RUNS!

She SOARS – *tch-tch-tch-tch* – to the top of the slippery slide. His wheels SQUEAL up the metal, but the heat causes them to skid right back down. He flops off. Fuming, he chucks rocks up at her. Big ones. Her bionic hand – *tch-tch-tch-tch* – CRUSHES them.

He scrambles up the ladder to reach her, she JUMPS! Her bionic arm —*tch-tch-tch-tch* – picks up that black two-wheeled terror and THRASHES it over and over on the scorching bitumen – *tch-tch-tch-tch* – counting to herself the number of times he's scared her, hurt her, terrified her. Her bionic legs STOMP – *tch-tch-tch-tch* – on the remaining mutilated metal. She takes what's left, SPRINTING – *tch-tch-tch-tch* – to the tipi, crouching, flicking her hair behind her bionic ear – *tch-tch-tch-tch* – he's getting close, very close. She waits.

Closer.

Closer.

Closer.

Now!

She SMASHES his face with the crushed metal. She's knocked him out.

She panics. Starts to shake him.

Shake!

Shake!

Wake!

Wake!

Boyanna can feel the blood in her mouth. She can't move, her elbows are stuck under her ribs, her palms are grazed and hurt like hell. She lies exactly where his bike plowed into her.

'You're alright Boy!' He laughs maniacally shouting over his shoulder 'Bye Bye Boy! See ya tomorrow!'

As she swallows her blood she swears she'll climb out of that bathroom window earlier, much earlier.

The last time **Mara Blazic** wrote fiction was in high school when the Men Without Hats did the safety dance and Madonna was a virgin. She pursued a career in facts instead and spent twenty-five years in television journalism. In 2016 she enrolled in Creative Writing at the University of Adelaide and since then her short stories have been recognised internationally in the Atlantis Short Story Contest, the Bristol Short Story Prize and now in the Bath Short Story Award. She's thrilled 'Bionic Girl' is selected for the 2017 Bath Short Story Award Anthology. She lives in Adelaide, Australia.